PROOFS & THEORIES

PROOFS

&

THEORIES

Essays on Poetry

LOUISE GLÜCK

THE ECCO PRESS

THE ECCO PRESS
100 West Broad Street
Hopewell, New Jersey 08525
Published simultaneously in Canada by
Penguin Books Canada Ltd., Ontario
Printed in the United States of America

Some of the essays in this book first appeared in the following
publications: *Antaeus, Ironwood, Southern Review, Threepenny Review,
The Village Voice.*

"The Best American Poetry 1993: Introduction" was originally
published in *The Best American Poetry 1993*, edited by Louise Glück,
David Lehman, series editor. Charles Scribner's and Sons,
New York: 1993.

"The Dreamer and the Watcher" was originally published in
Singular Voices: American Poetry Today, edited by Stephen Berg.
Avon Books, New York: 1985.

"Death and Absence" was originally published in *The Generation of
2000: Contemporary American Poets* edited by William Heyen.
Ontario Review Press, Princeton: 1984.

Designed by Richard Oriolo

Library of Congress Cataloging-in-Publication Data

Glück, Louise, 1943–
Proofs & theories : essays on poetry / Louise Glück. -- 1st ed.
p.   cm.
1. Poetics.   I. Title.   II. Title: Proofs and theories.
PN1055.G54   1994
811'.54--dc20   94-9820
ISBN 0-88001-369-9

The text of this book is set in Perpetua

To Stephen Berg

ACKNOWLEDGMENTS

Special thanks to Wendy Lesser for her promptings and suggestions, and sure handed editing, and for the example of her own work; and to Michael Ryan, for one of many gifts in twenty-five years of deep friendship: the persistent suggestion I try the essay form. This book would not exist without them.

CONTENTS

CONTENTS

AUTHOR'S NOTE

I live half the year among academics. More accurately, I live that half year *with* academics, Williams College, where I teach, being unmanageably far from where I otherwise live. For more than a decade, I have boarded each fall with Meredith Hoppin and David Langston, a classicist and a professor of English. Gifts of the fates: a personal classicist, a personal general resource library. From these friends, as from my departmental colleagues, I have learned something of the passions that inform scholarly pursuits.

It is a commonplace among creative writers to assume that passion is exactly what the academic lacks: we live, we tell ourselves, turbulent, invested lives, whereas academics invest their narrower energies in a kind of historical tidying-up service, their zeal for detail compensating for lack of creative intensity. But the passion for knowledge I see among scholars is as much a quest as what drives any artist—it too seeks illumination, but the terms (and results) of illumination differ from the artist's.

I have learned, in these ten years, deep respect for scholarship: opinions and beliefs, no matter how compelling or moving, cannot answer to that name. The essays contained here are explorations and occasional pieces, some specifically commissioned, some the result of prolonged brooding on themes better treated in prose than in poetry. This latter group seemed to arise generally out of some objection: to a term, to an approach, to an underlying premise. The essays on my own work respond to the particular requirements of two anthologies, *Singular Voices* and *The Generation of 2,000*. A number of the more sweepingly speculative essays were written as lectures for the MFA Program for Writers at Warren Wilson College. All, though, however they participate in the scholar's inclination to meditation, wholly lack the scholar's taste for research. I wrote these essays as I would poems; I wrote from what I know, trying to undermine the known with intelligent questions. Like poems, they have been my education.

PROOFS & THEORIES

EDUCATION
OF THE
POET

The fundamental experience of the writer is helplessness. This does not mean to distinguish writing from being alive: it means to correct the fantasy that creative work is an ongoing record of the triumph of volition, that the writer is someone who has the good luck to be able to do what he or she wishes to do: to confidently and regularly imprint his being on a sheet of paper. But writing is not decanting of personality. And most writers spend much of their time in various kinds of torment: wanting to write, being unable to write; wanting to write differently, being unable to write differently. In a whole lifetime, years are spent waiting to be claimed by an idea. The only real exercise of will is negative: we have toward what we write the power of veto.

It is a life dignified, I think, by yearning, not made serene by sensations of achievement. In the actual work, a discipline, a service. Or, to utilize the metaphor of childbirth which seems never to die: the writer is the one who attends, who facilitates: the doctor, the midwife, not the mother.

I use the word "writer" deliberately. "Poet" must be used cautiously; it names an aspiration, not an occupation. In other words: not a noun for a passport.

It is very strange to want so much what cannot be achieved in life. The high jumper knows, at the instant after performance, how high he has been; his achievement can be measured both immediately and with precision. But for those of us attempting dialogue with the great dead, it isn't a matter of waiting: the judgment we wait for is made by the unborn; we can never, in our lifetimes, know it.

The profundity of our ignorance concerning the merit of what we do creates despair; it also fuels hope. Meanwhile, contemporary opinion rushes to present itself as the intelligent alternative to ignorance: our task is to somehow insulate ourselves from opinion in its terminal forms, verdict and directive, while still retaining alert receptiveness to useful criticism.

If it is improper to speak as a poet, it is equally difficult to speak on the subject of education. The point, I think, would be to speak of what has left indelible impressions. But I discover such impressions slowly, often long after the fact. And I like to think they are still being made, and the old ones still being revised.

The axiom is that the mark of poetic intelligence or vocation is passion for language, which is thought to mean delirious response to language's smallest communicative unit: to the word. The poet is supposed to be the person who can't get enough of words like "incarnadine." This was not my experience. From the time, at four or five or six, I first started reading poems, first thought of the poets I read as my companions, my predecessors—from the beginning I preferred the simplest vocabulary. What fascinated me were the possibilities of context. What I responded to, on the page, was the way a poem could liberate, by means of a word's setting, through subtleties of timing, of pacing, that word's full and surprising range of meaning. It seemed to me that simple language best suited this enterprise; such language, in being generic, is likely to contain the greatest and most dramatic variety of meaning within individual words. I liked scale, but I liked it invisible. I loved those poems that seemed so small on the page but that swelled in the mind; I didn't like the windy, dwindling kind. Not surprisingly, the sort of sentence I was drawn to, which reflected these tastes and native habit of mind, was paradox, which has the added advantage of nicely rescuing the dogmatic nature from a too moralizing rhetoric.

I was born into the worst possible family given this bias. I was born into an environment in which the right of any family member to complete the sentence of another was assumed. Like most of the people in that family, I had a strong desire to speak, but that desire was regularly frustrated: my sentences were, in being cut off, radically changed—transformed, not paraphrased. The sweetness of paradox is that its outcome cannot be anticipated: this ought to insure the attention of the audience. But in my family, all discussion was carried on in that single cooperative voice.

I had, early on, a very strong sense that there was no point to speech if speech did not precisely articulate perception. To my mother, speech was the socially acceptable form of murmur: its function was to fill a room with ongoing, consoling human sound. And to my father, it was performance and disguise. My response was silence. Sulky silence, since I never stopped wanting deferential attention. I was bent on personal distinction, which was linked, in my mind, to the making of sentences.

In other ways, my family was remarkable. Both my parents admired intellectual accomplishment; my mother, in particular, revered creative gifts. At a time when women were not, commonly, especially well educated, my mother fought to go to college; she went to Wellesley. My father was the first and only son among five daughters, the first child born in this country. His parents had come from Hungary; my grandfather was a better dreamer than administrator of the family land: when the crops failed and the cattle died, he came to America, opened a grocery store. By family legend, a just man, less forceful than his wife and daughters. Before he died, his little store was the last piece of real estate on a block being bought up by one of the Rockefellers. This was generally deemed remarkably good fortune, in that my grandfather could ask, now, any price at all—an attitude for which my grandfather had complete contempt. He would ask, he said, the fair price: by definition, the same for Mr. Rockefeller as for anyone else.

I didn't know my father's parents; I knew his sisters. Fierce women, in the main dogmatic, who put themselves through college and had, in the remote past, dramatic and colorful love lives. My father refused to compete which, in his family, meant he refused to go to school. In a family strong on political conscience but generally deficient in imagination, my father wanted to be a writer. But he lacked certain qualities: lacked the adamant need which makes it possible to endure every form of failure: the humiliation of being overlooked, the humiliation of being found moderately interesting, the unanswerable fear of doing work that, in the end, really isn't more than moderately interesting, the discrepancy, which even the great writers live with (unless, possibly, they attain great age) between the dream and the evidence. Had my father's need been more acute, he probably would have found a means to overcome his emotional timidity; in the absence of acute need, he lacked motive to fight that battle. Instead, he went into business with his brother-in-law, made a notable success and lived, by most criteria, a full and fortunate life.

Growing up, I pitied him his decision. I think now that, in regard to my father, I'm blind, because I see in him my own weaknesses. But what my father needed to survive was not writing, it was belief in his potential—that he chose not to test that potential may have been good judgment, not, wholly, want of courage.

My mother was a sort of maid-of-all-work moral leader, the maker of policy. She considered my father the inspired thinker. She was dogged; he had that quality of mind my mother lacked, which she equated with imaginative capacity: he had lightness, wit. My mother was the judge. It was she who read my poems and stories and, later, the essays I wrote for school; it was her approval I lived on. It wasn't easy to get, since what my sister and I did was invariably weighed against what, in my mother's view, we had the ability to do. I used to regularly make the mistake of asking her what she thought. This was intended as a cue for praise, but my mother responded to the letter, not the spirit: always, and in detail, she told me exactly what she thought.

Despite these critiques, my sister and I were encouraged in every gift. If we hummed, we got music lessons. If we skipped, dance. And so on. My mother read to us, then taught us to read very early. Before I was three, I was well grounded in the Greek myths, and the figures of those stories, together with certain images from the illustrations, became fundamental referents. My father told stories. Sometimes these were wholly invented, like the adventures of a pair of bugs, and sometimes they were revised history, his particular favorite being the tale of St. Joan, with the final burning deleted.

My sister and I were being raised, if not to save France, to recognize and honor and aspire to glorious achievement. We were never given to believe that such achievement was impossible, either to our sex or our historical period. I'm puzzled, not emotionally but logically, by the contemporary determination of women to write as women. Puzzled because this seems an ambition limited by the existing conception of what, exactly, differentiates the sexes. If there are such differences, it seems to me reasonable to suppose that literature reveals them, and that it will do so more interestingly, more subtly, in the absence of intention. In a similar way, all art is historical: in both its confrontations and evasions, it speaks of its period. The dream of art is not to assert what is already known but to illuminate what has been hidden, and the path to the hidden world is not inscribed by will.

I read early, and wanted, from a very early age, to speak in return. When, as a child, I read Shakespeare's songs, or later, Blake and Yeats and Keats and Eliot, I did not feel exiled, marginal. I felt, rather, that this was the tradition of my language: *my* tradition, as English was my language. My inheritance. My wealth. Even before they've been lived through, a child can sense the great human subjects: time which breeds loss, desire, the world's beauty.

Meanwhile, writing answered all sorts of needs. I wanted to make something. I wanted to finish my own sentences. And I was sufficiently addicted to my mother's approval to want to shine at something she held in high esteem. When I wrote, our wishes coincided. And this was essential: hungry as I was for praise, I was also proud and could not bear to ask for it, to seem to need it.

Because I remember, verbatim, most of what I've written in the course of my life, I remember certain of my early poems; where written records exist, they confirm these memories. Here's one of the earliest, written around the time I was five:

> If kitty cats liked roastbeef bones
> And doggies sipped up milk;
> If elephants walked around the town
> All dressed in purest silk;
> If robins went out coasting,
> They slid down, crying whee,
> If all this happened to be true
> Then where would people be?

Plainly, I loved the sentence as a unit: the beginning of a preoccupation with syntax. Those who love syntax less find in it the stultifying air of the academy: it is, after all, a language of rules, of order. Its opposite is music, that quality of language which is felt to persist in the absence of rule. One possible idea behind such preferences is the fantasy of the poet as renegade, as the lawless outsider. It seems to me that the idea of lawlessness is a romance, and romance is what I most struggle to be free of.

I experimented with other mediums. For a while, I thought of painting, for which I had a small gift. Small but, like my other aptitudes, relentlessly developed. At some point in my late teens I realized I was at the end of what I could imagine on canvas. I think that, had my gift been larger or more compelling, I would still have found the visual arts a less congenial language. Writing suits the conservative temperament. What is edited can be preserved. Whereas the painter who recognizes that, in the interest of the whole, a part must be sacrificed, loses that part forever: it ceases to exist, except insofar as memory, or photographs, reproduce it. I couldn't bear the endless forfeits this involved; or perhaps I lack sufficient confidence in my immediate judgments.

In other ways as well, my preferences have not much changed. I experience, as a reader, two primary modes of poetic speech. One, to the reader, feels like confidence; one seems intercepted meditation. My preference, from the beginning, has been the poetry that requests or craves a listener. This is Blake's little black boy, Keats' living hand, Eliot's Prufrock, as opposed, say, to Stevens' astonishments. I don't intend, in this, to set up any sort of hierarchy, simply to say that I read to feel addressed: the complement, I suppose, of speaking in order to be heeded. There are exceptions, but the general preference remains intact.

The preference for intimacy, of course, makes of the single reader an elite. A practical advantage to this innate preference is that one cares less about the size of an audience. Or maybe the point here is that the writer's audience is chronological. The actor and dancer perform in the present; if their work exists in the future it exists as memory, as legend. Whereas the canvas, the bronze, and, more durably because they exist in multiple, the poem, the sonata, exist not as memory but as fact; the artists who work in these forms, scorned or overlooked in their own time, can still find an audience.

Among other profound divisions in literary taste, there's much talk currently about closure, about open-ended form, the idea being that such form is distinctly feminine. More interesting to me is a larger difference of which this is an example: the difference between symmetry and asymmetry, harmony and assonance.

I remember an argument I had with someone's mother when I was eight or nine; it was her day for carpool duty and our assignment in school had involved composition. I'd written a poem, and was asked to recite it, which I readily did. My special triumph with this poem had involved a metrical reversal in the last line (not that I called it that), an omission of the final rhyme: to my ear it was exhilarating, a kind of explosion of form. The form, of course, was doggerel. In any case, our driver congratulated me: a very good poem, she said, right till the last line, which she then proceeded to rearrange aloud into the order I had explicitly intended to violate. You see, she told me, all that was missing was that last rhyme. I was furious, and especially furious in that I knew my objections would read as defensive response to obvious failure.

It seems sometimes very strange to me, that image of a child so wholly bent on a vocation. So ambitious. The nature of that ambition, of literary ambition, seems to me a subject too large for this occasion. Like most people hungry for praise and ashamed of that, of any hunger, I alternated between contempt for the world that judged me and lacerating self-hatred. To my mind, to be wrong in the smallest particular was to be wrong utterly. On the surface, I was poised, cool, indifferent, given to laconic exhibitions of disdain. A description, I suppose, of any adolescence.

The discrepancy between what I would show the world and the chaos I felt grew steadily more intense. I wrote and painted, but these activities were hardly the famous release of such pressure they are contended to be. I cared too much about the quality of what I made; the context in which I judged what I made was not the schoolroom, but the history of art. In mid-adolescence, I developed a symptom perfectly congenial to the demands of my spirit. I had great resources of will and no self. Then, as now, my thought tended to define itself in opposition; what remains characteristic now was in those days the single characteristic. I couldn't say what I was, what I wanted, in any day to day, practical way. What I could say was *no:* the way I saw to separate myself, to establish a self with clear boundaries, was to oppose myself to the declared desire of others, utilizing their wills to give shape to my own. The conflict played itself out most fiercely with my mother. Insofar as I could tell, my mother only wavered when I began to refuse food, when I claimed, through implicit threat, ownership of my body, which was her great accomplishment.

The tragedy of anorexia seems to me that its intent is not self-destructive, though its outcome so often is. Its intent is to construct, in the only way possible when means are so limited, a plausible self. But the sustained act, the repudiation, designed to distinguish the self from the other also separates self and body. Out of terror at its incompleteness and ravenous need, anorexia constructs a physical sign calculated to manifest disdain for need, for hunger, designed to appear entirely free of all forms of dependency, to appear complete, self-contained. But the sign it trusts is a physical sign, impossible to sustain by mere act of will, and the poignance of the metaphor rests in this: that anorexia proves not the soul's superiority to but its dependence on flesh.

By the time I was sixteen, a number of things were clear to me. It was clear that what I had thought of as an act of will, an act I was perfectly capable of controlling, of terminating, was not that; I realized that I had no control over this behavior at all. And I realized, logically, that to be 85, then 80, then 75 pounds was to be thin; I understood that at some point I was going to die. What I knew more vividly, more viscerally, was that I didn't want to die. Even then, dying seemed a pathetic metaphor for establishing a separation between myself and my mother. I knew, at the time, very little about psychoanalysis; certainly, in those days, it was less common than now, in this era of proliferating therapies. Less common even in the affluent suburbs.

My parents, during these months, were wise enough to recognize that any suggestion they made I'd be committed to rejecting; therefore, they made no suggestions. And finally, one day, I told my mother I thought perhaps I should see a psychoanalyst. This was nearly thirty years ago—I have no idea where the idea, the word, came from. Nor was there, in those days, any literature about anorexia—at least, I knew of none. If there had been, I'd have been stymied; to have a disease so common, so typical, would have obliged me to devise some entirely different gestures to prove my uniqueness.

I was immensely fortunate in the analyst my parents found. I began seeing him in the fall of my senior year of high school; a few months later, I was taken out of school. For the next seven years, analysis was what I did with my time and with my mind; it would be impossible for me to speak of education without speaking of this process.

I was afraid of psychoanalysis in conventional ways. I thought what kept me alive, in that it gave me hope, was my ambition, my sense of vocation; I was afraid to tamper with the mechanism. But a certain rudimentary pragmatism told me that I had not yet accomplished a body of work likely to endure; therefore I couldn't afford to die. In any case, I felt I had no choice, which was a piece of luck. Because at seventeen I was not wild, not volcanic, I was rigid and self-protective; the form my self-protectiveness took was exclusion: that which I feared, I ignored; what I ignored, most of my central feelings, was not present in my poems. The poems I was writing were narrow, mannered, static; they were also other-worldly, mystical. These qualities were entirely defining. What was worse: by the time I began analysis, I'd stopped writing. So there was nothing, really, to protect.

But periodically, in the course of those seven years, I'd turn to my doctor with the old accusation: he'd make me so well, so whole, I'd never write again. Finally, he silenced me; the world, he told me, will give you sorrow enough. I think he waited to say that because, at the outset, the fact that the world existed at all was beyond me, as it is beyond all egotists.

Analysis taught me to think. Taught me to use my tendency to object to articulated ideas on my own ideas, taught me to use doubt, to examine my own speech for its evasions and excisions. It gave me an intellectual task capable of transforming paralysis—which is the extreme form of self-doubt—into insight. I was learning to use native detachment to make contact with myself, which is the point, I suppose, of dream analysis: what's utilized are objective images. I cultivated a capacity to study images and patterns of speech, to see, as objectively as possible, what ideas they embodied. Insofar as I was, obviously, the source of those dreams, those images, I could infer these ideas were mine, the embodied conflicts, mine. The longer I withheld conclusion, the more I saw. I was learning, I believe, how to write, as well: not to have a self which, in writing, is projected into images. And not, simply, to permit the production of images, a production unencumbered by mind, but to use the mind to explore the resonances of such images, to separate the shallow from the deep, and to choose the deep.

It is fortunate that that discipline gave me a place to use my mind, because my emotional condition, my extreme rigidity of behavior and frantic dependence on ritual, made other forms of education impossible. In fact, for many years every form of social interaction seemed impossible, so acute was my shame. But there was, after the first year, one other form open to me, or one need more powerful than shame. At 18, instead of going to college as I had always assumed I would, I enrolled in Leonie Adams' poetry workshop at the school of General Studies at Columbia.

I've written elsewhere about the years that followed, about the two spent studying with Dr. Adams, and the many years with Stanley Kunitz. Here's a poem, written long afterward, which simply records a few of the dreams in which Kunitz figures:

FOUR DREAMS
CONCERNING THE MASTER

1. The Supplicant

S. is standing in a small room, reading to himself.
It is a privilege to see S.
alone, in this serene environment.
Only his hand moves, thoughtfully turning the pages.
Then, from under the closed door, a single hazelnut
rolls into the room, coming to rest, at length,
at S.'s foot. With a sigh, S. closes the heavy volume
and stares down wearily at the round nut. "Well," he says,
"what do you want now, Stevens?"

2. Conversation with M.

"Have you ever noticed," he remarked,
"that when women sleep
they're really looking at you?"

3. Noah's Dream

Where were you in the dream?
    The North Pole.

Were you alone?
    No. My friend was with me.

Which friend was that?
    My old friend. My friend the poet.

What were you doing?
    We were crossing a river. But the clumps of ice
    were far apart, we had to jump.

Were you afraid?
    Just cold. Our eyes filled up with snow.

And did you get across?
    It took a long time. Then we got across.

What did you do then, on the other side?
    We walked a long time.

And was the walk the end?
    No. The end was the morning.

4. Conversation with X.

"You," he said, "you're just like Eliot.
You think you know everything in the world
but you don't believe anything."

Much is said of what a teacher in a creative enterprise cannot
do. Whatever they can't do, what they can do, the whole experience
of apprenticeship, seems to me beyond value. I was working, of

course, with extraordinary minds. And I was being exposed to images of dedication, not of the kind I knew, which I was not wholly prepared to comprehend. The poetic vocation is felt to be dramatic, glamorous; this is in part because consecration, which is dynamic, is so often mistaken for dedication. My notions of persistence were necessarily limited by youth. I was being shown, though, what it looked like, a steady upward labor; I was in the presence of that stamina I would find necessary. And I was privileged in feeling the steady application of scrutiny—from outside, from the world, from another human being. One of the rare, irreplaceable gifts of such apprenticeships is this scrutiny; seldom, afterward, is any poem taken with such high seriousness. Those of us trained in this environment have felt, I think, deeply motivated to provide for one another a comparable readership, and that need, founded so long ago, helps fend off the animosities, the jealousies, to which most of us are prone.

I was writing, in those years, with the inspiration of those teachers, those readers, the poems that were collected in my first book.

And if I had, as yet, no idea what kind of patience would be called for in my life, I had, by that time, already ample experience of what is called "writer's block." Though I hated the condition, a sense that the world had gone gray and flat and dull, I came to mistrust the premise behind the term. To be more precise: I can make sense of that premise in only two ways. It makes sense to presume fluency when the basis of the work is some intuition about language profound enough to be explored over a lifetime. Or when the work is anecdotal in nature. Even for the writer whose creative work arises out of the act of bearing witness—even for such a writer, a subject, a focus, must present itself, or be found. The artist who bears witness begins with a judgment, though it is moral, not aesthetic. But the artist whose gift is the sketch, the anecdote: that artist makes, as far as I can tell, no such judgment; nothing impedes the setting down of detail, because there is no investment in the idea of importance. When the aim of the work is spiritual insight, it seems absurd to expect fluency. A metaphor for such work is the oracle, which needed to be fed questions. In practical terms, this means that the writer who means to outlive the useful rages and despairs of youth must somehow learn to endure the desert.

I have wished, since I was in my early teens, to be a poet; over a period of more than thirty years, I have had to get through extended silences. By silences I mean periods, sometimes two years in duration, during which I have written nothing. Not written badly, written nothing. Nor do such periods feel like fruitful dormancy.

It seems to me that the desire to make art produces an ongoing experience of longing, a restlessness sometimes, but not inevitably, played out romantically, or sexually. Always there seems something ahead, the next poem or story, visible, at least, apprehensible, but unreachable. To perceive it at all is to be haunted by it; some sound, some tone, becomes a torment—the poem embodying that sound seems to exist somewhere already finished. It's like a lighthouse, except that, as one swims toward it, it backs away.

That's my sense of the poem's beginning. What follows is a period of more concentrated work, so called because as long as one is working the thing itself is wrong or unfinished: a failure. Still, this engagement is absorbing as nothing else I have ever in my life known. And then the poem is finished, and at that moment, instantly detached: it becomes what it was first perceived to be, a thing always in existence. No record exists of the poet's agency. And the poet, from that point, isn't a poet anymore, simply someone who wishes to be one.

In practical terms, this has meant having a good deal of unused time; I came to teaching reluctantly, twenty-five years ago.

My experience as a student taught me a profound gratitude, a sense of indebtedness. In the days when teaching jobs began to be possible to me, when, to support myself, I worked as a secretary in various offices, I feared teaching. I feared that, in the presence of a poem that seemed nearly remarkable, my competitiveness would seek to suppress the remarkable, not draw it out. What I saw when, during one of my most difficult silences, I finally began to teach was that at such moments authorship matters not at all; I realized that I felt compelled to serve others' poems in the same way, with the same ferocity, as I felt compelled to serve my own. It mattered to get the poem right, to get it memorable, toward which end nothing was held back. In this act, all the forces in my nature I least approve, the competitiveness, the envy, were temporarily checked. Whatever benefits accrued to individual poems through this activity, the benefits to me proved enormous. I found an activity in which to feel myself benign, helpful—that, obviously. But I had also discovered that I need not myself be writing to feel my mind work. Teaching became, for me, the prescription for lassitude. It doesn't always work, of course, but it has worked often enough, and steadily enough. On that first occasion, it worked miraculously quickly.

I'd moved to Vermont, taken a three month job at Goddard. I'd written one book, and then nothing in the two years following its publication. I began teaching in September; in September, I began writing again, writing poems entirely different from those in *Firstborn.*

This difference was intended, at least hoped for. What you learn organizing a book, making of a pile of poems an arc, a shaped utterance, is both exhilarating and depressing: as you discern the book's themes, its fundamental preoccupations, you see as well the poems' habitual gestures, those habits of syntax and vocabulary, the rhythmic signatures which, ideally, give the volume at hand its character but which it would be dangerous to repeat.

Each book I've written has culminated in a conscious diagnostic act, a swearing off. After *Firstborn,* the task was to make latinate suspended sentences, and to figure out a way to end a poem without sealing it shut. Since the last poems of *The House on Marshland* were written concurrently with the earliest poems in *Descending Figure,* the latter seems more difficult to speak of independently. I wanted to learn a longer breath. And to write without the nouns central to that second book; I had done about as much as I could with moon and pond. What I wanted, after *Descending Figure,* was a poem less perfect, less stately; I wanted a present tense that referred to something more fluent than the archetypal present. And then, obviously, the task was to write something less overtly heroic, something devoid of mythic reference.

This is far too compressed a synopsis to be accurate, but it will give a sense, I hope, of some compulsion to change, a compulsion not, perhaps, actually chosen. I see in this gesture the child I was, unwilling to speak if to speak meant to repeat myself.

—*The annual "Education of the Poet" Lecture at the Solomon R. Guggenheim Museum, New York City, January 31, 1989.*

ON T. S. ELIOT

Among the major literary figures of the early twentieth century, T.S. Eliot seems to be, in aesthetic terms, the easiest target. The charges against him, cumulatively, make him out to be the enemy of the life force. What characterizes the life force appears to be improvisation, variety, frankness, vigor, personality, some version of the common touch, some sense of communal affiliation. Or, alternatively, the kind of linguistic inventiveness which can be taken as the thriving organism's throwing off of constraints. The opposite of the life force is the classroom.

These charges were given pithy expression by William Carlos Williams, who might or might not be happy to find his own distastes currently institutionalized. Which is to say, it's Williams who is taught eagerly, by both scholars and poets, whereas Eliot is taught with animosity or pity. At least, this is my impression. I find what seem to be manifestations of a pressure to choose very interesting, since an advantage of literature over life is that the heart of the reader can be given wholly and simultaneously, even to writers who detested each other. But Williams's hold on readers often seems what he wanted his hold on Pound to be: absolute. Meanwhile, response to

Eliot seems not unlike response to Milton, response to anything that seems to be both irreproachable and unfriendly. It is also possible that Eliot's particular spirituality, his intense wish to be divested of temporal facts, may seem to contemporary readers not simply irresponsible but immoral: an indulgence of privilege and omen of our collective ruin.

I love both these poets, all the time. It may be useful to say a little more about Williams. The democratic expansiveness of the poems may not have found a parallel, in the life, in broad tolerance. New Jersey was a refuge. But it was the *correct* refuge; it could be called real life. Williams had a villager's suspicion of the alien: his genius made art out of the village, but his broader perceptions seem a little cranky, a little petulant. He took things personally: this was the glory of his work; it was also, from time to time, a limitation of character. Williams's hunger for Pound's favor was not necessarily the source of his dislike of Eliot, but it raised dislike to the level of rage.

That Williams didn't like Eliot is hardly surprising. Williams did not found the cult of the apparent, but he practised it as well as any poet I can name. He had a moral commitment to the actual, which meant the visible, whereas it was Eliot's compulsion to question that world. 'Unreal city' as opposed, say, to *January Morning*. It is important to keep in mind the fact that Eliot was human: this accounts for the helplessness in his verse. If Williams thought of the real as that which was capable of being registered by the senses, Eliot, in his deepest being, equated the real with the permanent. Under which system, earth does not qualify. To be human and feel this is to have certain fond attachments seriously undermined.

Among the great figures of the time, Eliot was, in the work, the least materialistic, the least consoled by the physical world. Because what he wanted was either to see through the material to the eternal (in which case the material was an obstacle to vision) or to experience a closing of the gap between the two worlds. Only through the closing of that gap between the actual and the ideal could the physical world attain meaning, authority. But a mind sensitive to this discrepancy is unlikely to experience a convincing union of these realms.

The impulse of our century has been to substitute earth for god as an object of reverence. This seems an implicit rejection of the eternal. But the religious mind, with its hunger for meaning and disposition to awe, its craving for the path, the continuum, the unbroken line, for what is final, immutable, cannot sustain itself on matter and natural process. It feels misled by matter; as for the anecdotes of natural process, these it transforms to myth. Reading Eliot and Williams in juxtaposition, you see something more profound than an aesthetic disagreement. Both write poems as speech (which is why Eliot never seems to me *literary*), but communication in Williams is not designed to forge enduring bonds between one being and another. What Williams values is energy; he is effervescent, many-mooded: on occasion, didactic, but at other times, sublimely unconcerned to be heard. The absence of the twin, the exact counterpart, authenticates his experience. Williams's speech remarks the immediate; it has confidence, animation, gusto. In this kind of speech, *living* and *dead* are the critical distinctions. For Eliot, there were other distinctions: *true* and *false*, for example, or the distinction between a single *right* and a proliferation of *wrongs*. Where variety interests Williams, choice is Eliot's obsession. And every choice is vulnerable to some absolute, external judgment. This explains, in part, the fastidious hesitations: when the compulsion of speech is to find and say the truth, which is single because inclusive, all utterance must be tormented by doubt. The capacity of such a mind for suffering has to be enormous.

In Williams, loneliness is a song. Williams, on the page, is not so much intimate as natural; he expects to be understood. Eliot begs. The anxiety of the need and the anguish of effort make for a desperate intimacy; as powerful a bond as can be imagined is created with the reader. Very different from the Roosevelt intimacies of Whitman, the monolith with the microphone, just as Eliot's austere spirituality is different from, say, Rilke's abandon. To read Eliot, for me, is to feel the presence of the abyss; to read Rilke is to sense the mattress under the window. The addiction to rapture seems, finally, less a form of abandon than of self-protection.

The goal, in Eliot's monologues, is communion. The problem is that an other cannot be found, or attention secured. Almost all the poems are beset by caution. Sentences falter; major ideas are regularly subordinated, delayed, qualified—Eliot's speakers either can't speak or can't be heard; their persistence makes the poems urgent.

I read this poetry for the first time as an adolescent. And understood it immediately, by which I mean I felt a connection to it. I heard the tone. If there is a criticism to make, it may come out of that: not that the work is 'academic', whatever that means, but that in the intensity and unchangingness of its emotion it is adolescent. And I suppose that, among sensitive readers, there must be many who do not share my taste for outcry. As an adult, I discovered that there is felt to be a division, in the Eliot *oeuvre,* marked by his conversion. The poems continue to seem to me more alike than they are different, the impact of the conversion not so very great. What has driven these poems from the first is terror and need of the understandable other. When the terror becomes unbearable, the other becomes god.

THE IDEA OF
COURAGE

Occasionally, discreetly, a new encomium introduces itself into the critical vocabulary. Not a new theory, which makes, necessarily, a more splendid debut, being, like all comprehensive visions, explicitly corrective, fueled by the ancient human impulse to reform. The process I mean to discuss is more covert: if not covert, unconscious, and the particular term under scrutiny one much more likely to be used (in my experience) by the poets themselves than by critics.

Poets have something to gain by giving currency to the idea of courage. In a solipsistic culture, no criterion of objectivity checks the need driving such analysis: when the world mirrors the self, recognition is experienced as a claim. Repeated use, moreover, lends to any terminology certain totemic properties: around a single word, brotherhoods and sisterhoods are created, the word itself coming to stand for all jointly held ambition and affirmed belief.

That courage animates a body of work seems, as an idea, immensely attractive. It dignifies the materials, infusing them with qualities of urgency and danger. In the ensuing confrontation, the poet becomes Perseus slaying the Medusa. Equally appealing is unconscious, helpless courage: Cassandra who cannot help but see. This alternative carries the additional benefit of suggesting that truth and vision are costly, their purchase secured by sacrifice or loss. The glamor of these, and related, images stimulates the aspiring visionary, who need simply reproduce the outward sign to invoke the spiritual condition: in this instance, need simply arrange to have paid.

Obviously, my focus here is narrow: courage takes on a more pointed meaning in more oppressive societies, societies in which it is literally not safe to speak. As is often noted, art benefits in such regimes (though artists do not) in that it acquires immense prestige, a prestige American poets may quite reasonably envy. But reasonable envy does not excuse muddled thought, nor can assertion of another, more amorphous species of courage convincingly argue the issue of peril.

In its local use, the term "courage" responds to poetic materials felt to be personal: in so doing, it concentrates attention on the poet's relation to his materials and to his audience, rather than on the political result of speech. Its obligation as analysis is to suggest analogues for exile and death: to name what is at risk.

Courage, in this usage, alludes to a capacity for facing down the dark forces. (Lust for generalization ignores the fact that not all people fear the same things.) From time to time, some permutation of the term acknowledges a range of essentially combative tones, tones one hears, say, in Lawrence (who uses them brilliantly): picking fights with the readers seems weirdly daring (and, by inference, courageous) in its apparent disdain for poetry's single reward, namely approval. In an extension of this reasoning, courage is also accorded the writer who makes some radical change of style and so courts disfavor. Present use of the term cannot be restricted to that poetry which arises out of genuine acts of physical or moral courage, perhaps because examples of such courage are so rare, perhaps because most examples seem corrupted by any first-person account, perhaps because the occasions themselves seem suspect, tainted by an air of contrivance. Ultimately, however, the point is that this sort of definition will not extend the uses of the term, and it is exactly this extension most poets desire. The need for incentive runs deep: the free society, the society that neither restricts speech nor values it, ennervates by presenting too few obstacles.

Desire notwithstanding, these assertions misunderstand the act of writing and, as well, the nature of courage.

No matter what the materials, the act of composition remains, for the poet, an act, or condition, of ecstatic detachment. The poems' declared subject has no impact on this state; however assessment is subsequently revised, the poet engaged in the act of writing feels giddy exhilaration; no occasion in the life calls less for courage than does this.

What seems at issue is the discrepancy between the impression of exposure and the fact of distance. The poet, writing, is simultaneously soaked in his materials and unconstrained by them: personal circumstance may prompt art, but the actual making of art is a revenge on circumstance. For a brief period, the natural arrangement is reversed: the artist no longer acted upon but acting; the last word, for the moment, seized back from fate or chance. Control of the past: as though the dead martyrs were to stand up in the arena and say, "Suppose, on the other hand . . ." No process I can name so completely defeats the authority of event.

Such defeat naturally imbues the poem with an aura of triumph. And it may be that this encourages misreading: the exhilaration of victory—over confusion, blankness, inertia, as well as over the past—resembles in appearance the victory of courage over dark matter, or the victory of passionate spirit over the impediments of civilization.

In this misreading, the material, or civilization, stands for the adversary, whose identity, whether human, animal, or inanimate, physical courage must always specify. Courage implies jeopardy, and jeopardy to the body depicts itself in correspondingly concrete terms. Whereas spiritual jeopardy, being invisible, lends itself to more speculative discourse, conception of the adversary growing very easily abstract.

But questions persist. If courage informs a poem of personal revelation, what, or who, is the adversary? What is at risk?

And the ready answer is: the possibility of shame. But it seems to me that no presumed confession, no subtle or explicit exposure, no ferocity of tone, no brazen (or compelled) shift in style can, through the mediation of the reader, transform the poem into an occasion which truly risks shame.

The empowering distance of the poet from his materials repeats itself in another equally useful distance: that of the poem from its reader. That the poem, that art, makes a bridge between one being and another—this commonplace perception—says as much: no bridge is necessary in the absence of distance. Inherently, the dynamic of shame depends on response: but response, for the poet, to the poem, occurs later, in an elsewhere distant in time from the time of composition; for the duration of active composition, the poet remains insulated from the future as from the past. Insulated, consequently, from any real exposure, from any present source of censure or mockery. True, the act of writing posits a listener, that one-who-will-understand. But an idealized listener differs from any actual listener in that the actual listener cannot be controlled: only the latter is a legitimate threat.

At such remove, the artist seems enviably shameless (or courageous). This perception is not so much false as skewed: indeed, the artist is shameless, protected from all humiliation, all real source of shame—as shameless, as easy in the performance of nakedness, as a naked dancer, whom the stage similarly protects. This is not to say that the motive of speech is exhibitionism. But the fact remains: for the artist, no *contact* occurs. And there is no confession, no possibility of shame, in the absence of contact.

A case can be made that publication reinstates vulnerability, collapsing the distance between both poet and materials and poet and reader. This overlooks the artist's most stubborn dilemma, itself a corollary of distance: specifically, the impossibility of connecting the self one is in the present with the self that wrote. The gap is both absolute and immediate: toward a finished work, only the most tormented sense of relationship remains, not a sense of authorship at all. The work stands as a reprimand or reproach, a marker permanently fixing an unbearable distance, the distance between the remote artist self, miraculously fluent, accidentally, fleetingly perceptive, and the clumsy, lost self in the world. Critical assault of a finished work is painful in that it affirms present self-contempt. What it cannot do, either for good or ill, is wholly fuse, for the poet, the work and the self; the vulnerability of the poet to critical reception remains complicated by that fact. And the sting the poet may suffer differs from the risks of more immediate exposure: the ostensibly exposed self, the author, is, by the time of publication, out of range, out of existence, in fact.

As to the argument that courage informs certain radical shifts in style: the need to write is, after all, the wish to be caught up in an idea; for the writer, thinking and writing (like thinking and feeling) are synonyms. Style changes when one has got to the end, willingly or not, of a train of thought. The choice, then, is between another train of thought and the spiritual equivalent of lip-sync. In any case, to deal in the written word is to deal, at the conscious level, in the future. The reader lives there, and the artist of unusually powerful or unusually fragile ego will favor the long future over the immediate, in part because an accumulated audience offers greater possibility of response, in part as protection or insurance against the potential coldness of present readers (the hunger for revenge against circumstance translating easily to this set of conditions). Toward his critics, the artist harbors a defensive ace: knowledge that the future will erase the present. Not all writers possess in equal measure these preoccupations: that they are available at all, psychically, to diminish the force of critical judgment, separates the judgment of published work from the more annihilating judgments which can occur in actual contact.

Our claim on this particular fortifying virtue cannot be made regarding the act of writing. For poets, speech and fluency seem less an act of courage than a state of grace. The intervals of silence, however, require a stoicism very like courage; of these, no reader is aware.

ON GEORGE
OPPEN

Within the discipline of criticism, nothing is more difficult than praise. To speak of what you love—not admire, not know to be good, not find reasonably interesting, not feel briefly moved by or charmed by—to speak of such work is difficult because the natural correlatives of awe and reverence are not verbal.

I have been, for some time, trying to speak on paper of the work of George Oppen, with this overwhelming impediment. But tribute seems necessary: a way of affirming certain values.

As a reader, consequently as a writer, I am partial to most forms of voluntary silence. I love what is implicit or present in outline, that which summons (as opposed to imposes) thought. I love white space, love the telling omission, love lacunae, and find oddly depressing that which seems to have left out nothing. Such poetry seems to love completion too much, and like a thoroughly cleaned room, it paralyzes activity. Or, to use another figure, it lacks magnetism, the power to seem, simultaneously, whole and not final, the power to generate, not annul, energy.

George Oppen is a master of white space; of restraint, juxtaposition, nuance. His art, though exquisite in detail and scrupulously precise, attains to scope and grandeur through what seems, in some ways, a mastery of perspective:

Ah these are the poor,
These are the poor—

Bergen street.

There is something Oriental in this; what is, to my limited understanding, less Oriental is the momentum of the poems. Oppen has not got Williams' scampering vitality, but he seems Williams' celestial counterpart. A difference, it seems to me, is that Oppen's mind more craves abstraction (the gift for context, for perspective, being an example of this). Williams at his least good is stubbornly trivial; Oppen, at his least good, relentlessly lofty; he risks the tedium of the unrelievedly exhaulted.

The self, in Oppen as in Williams, is a source of information. The individual life, frail, awkward, imperfect, is at every moment the vessel which contains the soul or mind, and it is about the mind, in particular, that Oppen speaks with greatest ardor, infusing mind with radiant spiritual properties:

The virtue of the mind
Is that emotion
Which causes
To see

Very odd, that sentence, that "causes to see." There seems a deleted noun or pronoun, in the absence of which "to see" explodes as the object of "causes." The individual self is a location, its presence implicit. Only in a specific self can "the virtue of mind" produce a concrete result. Immediately, the poem moves on: what would be, in another poet, solemn conclusion becomes in Oppen a development.

There is a powerful sense, in this poetry, of that which is precious: what is precious to Oppen is usually singular, common, and small. Thus the concern not for *language* so much as *words*:

> Possible
> To use
> Words provided one treats them
> As enemies. . . .

Possible, that is

> . . . If one captures them
> One by one proceeding
>
> Carefully they will restore
> I hope to meaning
> And to sense.

How beautiful that last word, how typically direct and practical. This is Oppen's definition of substance and integrity. This particular ideal of service to language carries with it a high valuation of communication. Very different from the service done, say, by Stevens, with his taste for rarities, his autoerotic sensuousness. Words restored, according to Oppen's criteria, to natural health and soundness make a language available for common use, not a hermetic patois. If "meaning" and "sense" seem insufficiently charged for poetry, so much the better; they remind us that precision is not the opposite of mystery.

These are Olympian sentiments, for all the prizing of simplicities. But the lines themselves are neither condescending nor didactic; the "I" here is the author of a prayer that seems remarkably poignant, as "hope" seems fragile among such solid nouns. There is nothing in Oppen of romantic swagger, of the diva, the "I, David, will do this with my little slingshot."

Moral passion usually manifests itself in decisiveness, which becomes a compulsion to take sides. But a mind either intensely religious or unusually open may invest such passion in acts of speculation. These poems speak a moral language, a language of salvation and contempt: they have the force of true passion, but none of the smarmy definitiveness, none of the self-righteousness. Their beauty has always seemed to me the beauty of logic, the "virtue of the mind", whose end is vision:

> . . . we walked
> To where it would have wet our feet
> Had it been water

AGAINST
SINCERITY

S ince I'm going to use inexplicit terms, I want to begin by defining
the three most prominent of these. By *actuality* I mean to refer to
the world of event, by *truth* to the embodied vision, illumination, or
enduring discovery which is the ideal of art, and by *honesty* or *sincer-
ity* to "telling the truth," which is not necessarily the path to
illumination.

V.S. Naipaul, in the pages of a national magazine, defines the
aim of the novel; the ideal creation, he says, must be "indistinguish-
able from truth." A delicious and instructive remark. Instructive be-
cause it postulates a gap between truth and actuality. The artist's task,
then, involves the transformation of the actual to the true. And the
ability to achieve such transformations, especially in art that presumes
to be subjective, depends on conscious willingness to distinguish truth
from honesty or sincerity.

The impulse, however, is not to distinguish but to link. In part
the tendency to connect the idea of truth with the idea of honesty is a
form of anxiety. We are calmed by answerable questions, and the
question "Have I been honest?" has an answer. Honesty and sincerity
refer back to the already known, against which any utterance can be

tested. They constitute acknowledgement. They also assume a convergence: these terms take for granted the identification of the poet with the speaker.

This is not to suggest that apparently honest poets don't object to having their creativity overlooked. For example, the work of Diane Wakoski fosters as intense an identification of poet with speaker as any body of work I can think of. But when a listener, some years ago, praised Wakoski's courage, Wakoski was indignantly dismissive. She reminded her audience that, after all, she decided what she set down. So the "secret" content of the poems, the extreme intimacy, was regularly transformed by acts of decision, which is to say, by assertions of power. The "I" on the page, the all-revealing Diane, was her creation. The secrets we choose to betray lose power over us.

To recapitulate: the source of art is experience, the end product truth, and the artist, surveying the actual, constantly intervenes and manages, lies and deletes, all in the service of truth. Blackmur talks of this: "The life we all live," he says, "is not alone enough of a subject for the serious artist; it must be a life with a leaning, life with a tendency to shape itself only in certain forms, to afford its most lucid revelations only in certain lights."

There is, unfortunately, no test for truth. That is, in part, why artists suffer. The love of truth is felt as chronic aspiration and chronic unease. If there is no test for truth, there is no possible security. The artist, alternating between anxiety and fierce conviction, must depend on the latter to compensate for the sacrifice of the sure. It is relatively easy to say that truth is the aim and heart of poetry, but harder to say how it is recognized or made. We know it first, as readers, by its result, by the sudden rush of wonder and awe and terror.

The association of truth with terror is not new. The story of Psyche and Eros tells us that the need to know is like a hunger: it destroys peace. Psyche broke Eros's single commandment—that she not look at him—because the pressure to see was more powerful than either love or gratitude. And everything was sacrificed to it.

We have to remember that Psyche, the soul, was human. The

legend's resolution marries the soul to Eros, by which union it—the soul—is made immortal. But to be human is to be subject to the lure of the forbidden.

Honest speech is a relief and not a discovery. When we speak of honesty, in relation to poems, we mean the degree to which and the power with which the generating impulse has been transcribed. Transcribed, not transformed. Any attempt to evaluate the honesty of a text must always lead away from that text, and toward intention. This may make an interesting trail, more interesting, very possibly, than the poem. The mistake, in any case, is our failure to separate poetry which sounds like honest speech from honest speech. The earlier mistake is in assuming that there is only one way for poetry to sound.

These assumptions didn't come from nowhere. We have not so much made as absorbed them, as we digest our fathers and turn to our contemporaries. That turning is altogether natural: in the same way, children turn to other children, the dying to the dying, and so forth. We turn to those who have been dealt, as we see it, roughly the same hand. We turn to see what they're up to, feeling natural excitement in the presence of what is still unfolding, or unknown. Substantial contributions to our collective inheritance were made by poets whose poems seemed blazingly personal, as though the poets had performed autopsies on their own living tissue. The presence of the speaker in these poems was overwhelming; the poems read as testaments, as records of the life. Art was redefined, all its ingenuities washed away.

The impulse toward this poetry is heard in poets as unlike as Whitman and Rilke. It is heard, earlier, in the Romantics, despite Wordsworth's comment that if he "had said out passions as they were, the poems could never have been published." But the idea that a body of work corresponds to and describes a soul's journey is particularly vivid in Keats. What we hear in Keats is inward listening, attentiveness of a rare order. I will say more later about the crucial difference between such qualities and the decanting of personality.

Keats drew on his own life because it afforded greatest access to the materials of greatest interest. That it was *his* hardly concerned him. It was a life, and therefore likely, in its large shapes and major struggles, to stand as a paradigm. This is the attitude Emerson means, I think, when he says: "to believe your own thought, to believe that what is true for you in your private heart is true for all men—that is genius."

That is, at any rate, Keats's genius. Keats wanted a poetry that would document the soul's journey or shed light on hidden forms; he wanted more feeling and fewer alexandrines. But nothing in Keats's attitude toward the soul resembles the proprietor's investment. We can find limitation, but never smug limitation. A great innocence sounds in the lines, a kind of eager gratitude that passionate dedication should have been rewarded with fluency. As in this sonnet, dated 1818:

WHEN I HAVE FEARS

When I have fears that I may cease to be
Before my pen has gleaned my teeming brain,
Before high-pilèd books in charact'ry,
Hold like rich garners the full-ripened grain;
When I behold, upon the night's starred face,
Huge cloudy symbols of a high romance,
And think that I may never live to trace
Their shadows, with the magic hand of chance;
And when I feel, fair creature of an hour!
That I shall never look upon thee more,
never have relish in the fairy power
of unreflecting love!—then on the shore
of the wide world I stand alone, and think
Till Love and Fame to nothingness do sink.

The impression is of outcry, of haste, of turbulent, immediate emotion that seems to fall, almost accidentally, into the sonnet form. That form tends to produce a sensation of repose; no matter how paradoxical the resolution, the ear detects something of the terminal thud of the judge's gavel. Or the double thud, since the sensation is especially marked in sonnets following the Elizabethan style, ending, that is, in a rhymed couplet; two pithy lines of summary or antithesis. "Think" and "sink" make, certainly, a noticeable rhyme, but they manage, oddly enough, not to end the sonnet like two pennies falling on a plate. We require the marked rhyme, the single repeated sound, to put an end to all the poem's surging longing, to show us the "I," the speaker, at a standstill, just as the dash in the twelfth line makes the necessary abyss that separates the speaker from all the richness of the world. Consider, now, another sonnet, akin to this in subject and rational shape, though the "when" and "then" are here more subtle. The sonnet is Milton's, its occasion, the fact of blindness, its date of composition, 1652:

WHEN I CONSIDER HOW MY LIGHT IS SPENT

When I consider how my light is spent
Ere half my days in this dark world and wide,
And that one talent which is death to hide
Lodged with me useless, though my soul more bent
To serve therewith my Maker, and present
My true account, lest He returning chide
"Doth God exact day-labor, light denied?"
I fondly ask. But Patience, to prevent
That murmur, soon replies, "God doth not need
Either man's work or his own gifts; who best
Bear His mild yoke, they serve Him best. His state
Is kingly: thousands at His bidding speed,
And post o'er land and ocean without rest:
They also serve who only stand and wait."

When I say the resemblance here is sufficient to make obvious the debt, what I mean is that I cannot read Keats's poem and not hear Milton's. Someone else would hear Shakespeare: neither echo is surprising. If Shakespeare was Keats's enduring love, Milton was his measuring rod. Keats carried a portrait of Shakespeare everywhere, even on the walking tours, as a kind of totem. When there was a desk, the portrait hung over it: work there was work at a shrine. Milton was the dilemma; toward Milton's achievement, Keats vacillated in his responses, and responses, to Keats, were verdicts. Such vacillation, combined with inner pressure to decide, can be called obsession.

The purpose of comparison was, finally, displacement; in Keats's mind, Wordsworth stood as the contender, the alternative. Keats felt Wordsworth's genius to lie in his ability to "[think] into the human heart"; Milton, for all his brilliance, showed, Keats thought, "less anxiety about humanity." Wordsworth was exploring those hidden reaches of the mind where, as Keats saw it, the intellectual problems of their time lay. And these problems seemed more difficult, more complex, than the theological questions with which Milton was absorbed. So Wordsworth was "deeper than Milton," though more because of "the general and gregarious advance of intellect, than individual greatness of mind." All this was a way for Keats of clarifying purpose.

I said earlier that these sonnets were like in their occasions: this statement needs some amplification. The tradition of sincerity grows out of the blurring of distinction between theme and occasion; there is a greater emphasis, after the Romantics, on choice of occasion: the poet is less and less the artisan who makes, out of an occasion tossed him, something of interest. The poet less and less resembles the debating team: lithe, adept, of many minds.

In the poems at hand, both poets have taken up the question of loss. Of course, Keats was talking about death, which remains, as long as one is talking, imminent. But pressingly imminent, for Keats, even in 1818. He had already nursed a mother through her dying and had watched her symptoms reappear in his brother Tom. Consumption was the "family disease"; Keats's medical training equipped him to recognize its symptoms. The death imminent to Keats was a forfeit of the physical world, the world of the senses. That world—this world—was heaven; in the other he could not believe, nor could he see his life as a ritual preparation. So he immersed himself in the momentary splendor of the material world, which led always to the idea of loss. That is, if we recognize movement and change but no longer believe in anything beyond death, then all evolution is perceived as movement away, the stable element, the referent, being what was, not what will be, a world as stationary and alive as the scenes on the Grecian urn.

In 1652, Milton's blindness was probably complete. Loss makes his starting place; if blindness is, unlike death, a partial sacrifice, it is hardly a propitiation: Milton's calm is not the calm of bought time. I say "Milton's" calm, but in fact, we don't feel quite so readily the right to that familiarity. For one thing, the sonnet is a dialogue, the octet ending in the speaker's question, which Patience answers in its six sublime lines. In a whole so fluent, the technical finesse of this division is masterfully inconspicuous. It is interesting to remark, of a poem so masterful, so majestic in its composure, the extreme simplicity of vocabulary. One-syllable words predominate; the impression of mastery derives not from elaborate vocabulary but from the astonishing variety of syntax within flexible suspended sentences, an instance of matchless organizational ability. People do not, ordinarily, speak this way. And I think it is generally true that imitations of speech, with its false starts, its lively inelegance, its sense of being arranged as it goes along, will not produce an impression of perfect control.

And yet there is, in Milton's poem, no absence of anguish. As readers, we register the anguish and drama here almost entirely subliminally, following the cues of rhythm. This is the great advantage of formal verse: metrical variation provides a subtext. It does what we now rely on tone to do. I should add that I think we really do have to rely on tone, since the advantage disappears when these conventions cease to be the norm of poetic expression. Education in metrical forms is not, however, essential to the reader here: the sonnet's opening lines summon and establish the iambic tradition, with a certain flutter at "consider." No ear can miss the measured regularity of those first lines:

> When I consider how my light is spent
> Ere half my days in this dark world and wide. . . .

The end of the second line, though, is troubled. "Dark world" makes a kind of aural knot. We hear menace not simply because the world is described as "dark," alluding both to the permanently altered world of the blind and, also, to a world metaphorically dark, in which right paths cannot be detected: the menace felt here comes about, and comes about chiefly, because the line that has been so fluid is suddenly stalled. A block is thrown up, the language itself coagulates into the immobile, impassable dark world. Then we escape; the line turns graceful again. But the dread introduced is not dissolved. And in the fourth line we hear it again with terrible force, so that we experience physically, in sound, the unmanageable sorrow:

> And that one talent which is death to hide
> Lodged with me useless. . . .

"Lodged" is like a blow. And the next words make a kind of lame reeling, a dwindling. As I hear the line, only "less" receives less emphasis than "me." In these four words we hear personal torment, the wreckage of order and hope; we are carried to a place as isolated as Keats's shore ever was, but a place of fewer options. All this happens early; Milton's sonnet is not a description of agony. But loss must be vividly felt for Patience's answer to properly reverberate.

The most likely transformation of loss is into task or test. This conversion introduces the idea of gain, if not reward; it fortifies the animal commitment to staying alive by promising to respond to the human need for purpose. So Patience, in Milton's sonnet, stills the petulant questioner and provides a glimpse of insight, a directive. At the very least, corrects a presumption.

Great value is placed here on endurance. And endurance is not required in the absence of pain. The poem, therefore, must convince us of pain, though its concerns lie elsewhere. Specifically, it proposes a lesson, which must be unearthed from the circumstantial. In the presence of lessons, the possibility of mastery can displace the animal plea for alleviation.

In Milton's sonnet, two actions are ascribed to the speaker: he considers, and, when he considers, he asks. I have made a particular case for anguish because we are accustomed to thinking the "cerebral" contradictory to the "felt," and the actions of the speaker are clearly the elevated actions of mind. The disposition to reflect or consider presumes developed intelligence, as well as temperamental inclination; it further presumes adequate time.

The "I" that considers is very different from the "I" that has fears. To have fears, to have, specifically, the fears on which Keats dwells, is to be immersed in acute sensation. The fear that one will cease to be is unlike the state of chronic fearfulness we call timidity. This fear halts and overtakes, it carries intimations of change or closure or collapse, it threatens to cancel the future. It is primal, unwilled, democratic, urgent; in its presence, all other function is suspended.

What we see in Keats is not indifference to thought. What we see is another species of thought than Milton's: thought resistant to government by mind. Keats claims for the responsive animal nature its ancient right to speech. Where Milton will project an impression of mastery, Keats projects a succumbing. In terms of tone, the impression of mastery and the impression of abandon cannot co-exist. Our present addiction to sincerity grows out of a preference for abandon, for the subjective "I" whose impassioned partiality carries the implication of flaw, whose speech sounds individual and human and fallible. The elements of coldness to which Keats objected in Milton, the insufficient "anxiety about humanity" correspond to the overt projection of mastery.

Keats was given to describing his methods of composition in terms implying a giving-in: the poet was to be passive, responsive, available to all sensation. His desire was to reveal the soul, but soul, to Keats, had no spiritual draperies. Spirituality manifests the mind's intimidating claim to independent life. It was this invention Keats rejected. To Keats, the soul was corporeal and vital and frail; it had no life outside the body.

Keats refused to value what he did not believe, and he did not believe what he could not feel. Because he saw no choice, Keats was bound to prefer the mortal to the divine, as he was bound to gravitate toward Shakespeare, who wrote plays where Milton made masks, who wrote, that is, with an expressed debt to life.

It follows that Keats's poems feel immediate, personal, exposed; they sound, in other words, exactly like honesty, following Wordsworth's notion that poetry should seem the utterance of "a man talking to men." If Milton wrote in momentous chords, Keats preferred the rush of isolated notes, preferred the penetrating to the commanding.

The idea of "a man talking to men," the premise of honesty, depends on a delineated speaker. And it is precisely on this point that confusion arises, since the success of such a poetry creates in its readers a firm belief in the reality of that speaker, which is expressed as the identification of the speaker with the poet. This belief is what the poet means to engender: difficulty comes when he begins to participate in the audience's mistake. And on this point, we should listen to Keats, who intended so plainly that his poems seem personal and who drew, so regularly and so unmistakably, on autobiographical materials.

At the center of Keats's thinking is the problem of self. And it is on the subject of the poet's self that he speaks with greatest feeling and insight. Those men of talent, he felt, who impose their "proper selves" on what they create, should be called "men of power," in contrast to the true "men of genius," those men who, in Keats's view, were "great as certain ethereal chemicals operating on the mass of neutral intellect—but they have not any individuality, any determined character." Toward the composition of poems that would seem "a man speaking to men," he advocated the opposite of egotistical self-awareness and self-cultivation; he recommended, rather, the negative capability he felt in Shakespeare, a capacity for suspending judgment in order to report faithfully, a capability of submission, a willingness to "annul" the self.

The self, in other words, was like a lightning rod: it attracted experience. But the poet's obligation was to divest himself of personal characteristics. Existing beliefs, therefore, were not a touchstone, but a disadvantage.

I referred, some time ago, to our immediate inheritance. I had in mind poets like Lowell and Plath and Berryman, along with many less impressive others. With reference to the notion of sincerity, it is especially interesting to look at Berryman.

Berryman was, from the first, technically proficient, though the early poems are not memorable. When he found what we like to call "himself," he demonstrated what is, to my mind, the best ear since Pound. The self he found was mordant, voluble, opinionated, and profoundly withheld, as demonically manipulative as Frost. In 1970, after *The Dream Songs* had made him famous, Berryman published a curious book, which took its title from the Keats sonnet. The book, *Love and Fame,* was dedicated "to the memory of the suffering lover & young Breton master who called himself 'Tristan Corbière.'" To this dedication, Berryman added a parenthetical comment: "I wish I versed with his bite."

We have, therefore, by the time we reach the first poem, a great deal of information: we have a subject, youth's twin dreams, a reference, and an ideal. But this is as nothing compared to the information we get in the poems. We get in them the kind of instantly gratifying data usually associated with drunken camaraderie, and not with art. We get actual names, places, positions, and, while Berryman is at it, confessions of failure, pride, ambition, and lust, all in characteristic shorthand: arrogance without apology.

It can be said of Berryman that when he found his voice he found his voices. By voice I mean natural distinction, and by distinction I mean to refer to thought. Which is to say, you do not find your voice by inserting a single adjective into twenty poems. Distinctive voice is inseparable from distinctive substance; it cannot be grafted on. Berryman began to sound like Berryman when he invented Mr. Bones, and so was able to project two ideas simultaneously. Presumably, in *Love and Fame,* we have a single speaker—commentator might be a better word. But the feel of the poems is very like that of *The Dream Songs;* Mr. Bones survives in an arsenal of sinister devices, particularly in the stinging, undermining tag lines. The poems pretend to be straight gossip, straight from the source; like gossip, they divert and entertain. But the source deals in mixed messages; midway through, the reader is recalled from the invited error:

MESSAGE

Amplitude,—voltage,—the one friend calls for the one,
the other for the other, in my work;
in verse & prose. Well, hell.
I am not writing an autobiography-in-verse, my friends.

Impressions, structures, tales, from Columbia in the thirties
& the michaelmas term at Cambridge in 36,
followed by some later. It's not my life.
That's occluded and lost.

On the page, "autobiography-in-verse" is a single ladylike word, held together by malicious hyphens.

What's real in the passage is despair. Which owes, in part, to the bitter notion that invention is wasted.

The advantage of poetry over life is that poetry, if it is sharp enough, may last. We are unnerved, I suppose, by the thought that authenticity, in the poem, is not produced by sincerity. We incline, in our anxiety for formulas, to be literal: we scan Frost's face compulsively for hidden kindness, having found the poems to be, by all reports, so much better than the man. This assumes our poems are our fingerprints, which they are not. And the processes by which experience is changed—heightened, distilled, made memorable—have nothing to do with sincerity. The truth, on the page, need not have been lived. It is, instead, all that can be envisioned.

I want to say, finally, something more about truth, or about that art which is "indistinguishable" from it. Keats's theory of negative capability is an articulation of a habit of mind more commonly ascribed to the scientist, in whose thought the absence of bias is actively cultivated. It is the absence of bias that convinces, that encourages confidence, the premise being that certain materials arranged in certain ways will always yield the same result. Which is to say, something inherent in the combination has been perceived.

I think the great poets work this way. That is, I think the materials are subjective, but the methods are not. I think this is so whether or not detachment is evident in the finished work.

At the heart of that work will be a question, a problem. And we will feel, as we read, a sense that the poet was not wed to any one outcome. The poems themselves are like experiments, which the reader is freely invited to recreate in his own mind. Those poets who claustrophobically oversee or bully or dictate response prematurely advertise the deficiencies of the chosen particulars, as though without strenuous guidance the reader might not reach an intended conclusion. Such work suffers from the excision of doubt: Milton may have written proofs, but his poems compel because they dramatize questions. The only illuminations are like Psyche's, who did not know what she'd find.

The true has about it an air of mystery or inexplicability. This mystery is an attribute of the elemental: art of the kind I mean to describe will seem the furthest concentration or reduction or clarification of its substance; it cannot be further refined without being changed in its nature. It is essence, ore, wholly unique, and therefore comparable to nothing. No "it" will have existed before; what will have existed are other instances of like authenticity.

The true, in poetry, is felt as insight. It is very rare, but beside it other poems seem merely intelligent comment.

ON HUGH SEIDMAN

Strictly speaking, *Collecting Evidence* may not be out of print: Unmuzzled Ox recently reissued it in an extremely limited edition. For what are plainly pressing financial reasons, this edition has something of an impromptu look, being simply a rudimentarily bound together sheaf of pages, Xeroxed from the original. If this version lacks the look and feel of a book, it nevertheless makes Hugh Seidman's remarkable first collection available to new readers.

Collecting Evidence was originally published in 1970, the first of Stanley Kunitz's extraordinary selections for the Yale Series. Difficult to imagine American poetry, the poetry of my generation, without the writers introduced during Kunitz's editorship, without, among others, Hass, Ryan, Forché, Stanton. The high reputation of those poets reflects their achievement, but reputation is not a reliable index of brilliance.

Hugh Seidman is terse in a period that admires discursiveness; when taste equates expansiveness with profundity, a poet so obsessive, so temperamentally austere, is unlikely to win praise. We live in an age of dogma: this encourages readers to mistake representation for advocacy. And the relentless pain of Seidman's work is sometimes read as stubborn repudiation of all that is warm, beautiful, wholesome, tender. We have, I think, great terror of pain, and consequent resistance to what it can teach. Twenty years after their publication, the anguish of these poems remains immediate, absolute, their content-driven, disruptive boldness utterly distinct from the meticulous terrorism of most contemporary formal experimentation. I know few collections so lacking in complacency, so adamant in their refusal to charm or console, so fiercely intelligent.

Detailed commentary is somewhat constrained by Kunitz's introduction, which is, like those that followed, dauntingly eloquent. Kunitz begins by comparing Seidman to Baudelaire, via Walter Benjamin's study, which "projects the image of the poet as detective, who . . . tirelessly explores the streets of the metropolis, scanning the behavior of the crowd for the sins of its secret guilts . . . " Seidman's investigator is particularly furtive, particularly driven, alert to his compulsions, paralyzingly alert to the implications of his actions:

> Venturing to the world:
> the doctor's office.
>
> The civilized diseases:
> gonorrhea, falling hair,
> bad skin, neurasthenia.
>
> Body edging into spirit
> and I debate:
> Is it moral to get better?

Like all Seidman's questions, inexhaustible because unanswerable. Hence the debate. And, too, paralysis, since it may be impossible to wish for wholeness and, at the same time, strive toward moral action. Few lines of poetry name a dilemma as succinctly, as tellingly; few as devastatingly specify the disease of an epoch. Behind this question lurk others concerning tribal affiliation, the requirements of civilization. And no poetry could be further from the poetry of noble sentiment, gracefully phrased. Typically, investigation focuses on the self, though, as the aptness of Kunitz's comparison suggests, these are hardly confessional poems; both tonally and formally, this is a world very different from, say Lowell's. At the center is the writhing self, but what characterizes Seidman's style is its strange objectivity, a hybrid of the camera's cool, compensatory voyeurism and the clinician's dispassion. Lowell, at his best, is heroic; Seidman, as Kunitz observes, is not. These are poems less of lack than of division, as the regular use of third person documents: the self, the specimen man, enacts his compulsions, linked to but not fused with the intelligence that records. The grandeur of the work lies not in its manner but in the immense distance between these selves, and in the complexity of their relation, simultaneously conflicted and symbiotic.

An aspect of relentless intelligence is that it finds no resting place (which may account for certain religious conversions, since the need for rest grows in proportion to the mind's relentlessness). I think of Oppen's lines: "And there are those/ In it so violent/ And so alone/ They cannot rest." Seidman resembles Oppen in his spare elegance and scope of his concerns, though not in temperament. Beside Oppen's unsanctimonious calm, Seidman seems a marked man: mortal, embattled, grimly, almost fetishistically erotic.

The poems' perspective on Eros is memory's: always the lover's body has been forbidden (a corroboration of existing self loathing) and the poet writes in an onanistic torment of sexual exile. Recreation of the beloved is, in the most literal sense, sullying: love, in these poems, is insane longing and pursuit of the past; it begins in and depends on the act of rejection. This is not an uncommon motivation in poetry, but few poets explore mortification so obsessively. Among those who do, almost none seek release from delusion.

> The black pigeon straggles under the parked car
> I feel the pain of the cracked wings
> I reach to it but it hides near the wheel
>
> Later I see the bloody and headless
> Half body of a pigeon lying in the street

The ease of such comparison persists
We struggle to survive these sentiments

Religion documents the relation of affliction to ecstasy. Poetry generated by suffering—perhaps, more precisely, poetry which is compelled to explore suffering as its principal subject—tends to produce moments of high recklessness or hallucination, a linguistic abandon that endows ecstasy with concrete form. If Seidman has less conspicuous virtuosity than Plath (to fix on the obvious contemporary example), he has, to my mind, greater subtlety, an inclination to prefer recalcitrant mystery to hallucination, though both aspects of this transformation occur in *Collecting Evidence*. Of "The Making of Color" Kunitz writes that here "color mounts on color, pigment on pigment, each in the semblance of its base ingredients, until we arrive at the extreme temperature of transubstantiation, as if the matter of the life were being converted into pure gold, pure fire, pure spiritual energy":

The pages are stained with purple
The letters are written in gold
The covers are encrusted with gems
St. Jerome remonstrates
The curling writhes
Molten gold on carbon
Ink burnt ash grey
Emerald into vapor
The book, the codex, the manuscript
The canvas, the panel, the wall,
Conflagrant world against world

Or, in the other mode, insights resistant to paraphrase, like the moment at the end of "Surreal Poem":

. . . . What else is there,
this falling into ourselves, as
thru the bathtub water, covered
with the film of mercury.

Or the lucid somnambulism of "Poem":

> How the Lord of Death came to lay his moist finger at my throat
> I went to the fork of the streets
> But the distances were different and had lengthened
> I heard the voices behind me as I ran
> And awoke to the leaves which were the wind
> Insane with tiredness and distant from myself
> And how I had awakened beside you years ago
> To fend away your touch turning in half sleep
> For the loss of love does not cease in this world

THE
FORBIDDEN

In the myth of the Garden, the forbidden exerts over the suscep-
tible human mind irresistible allure. The force of this allure is abso-
lute, final; the fact of it shapes, ever afterward, human character and
the human vision of human destiny. The myth's potency derives from
the fact that there is no going back: exile and contamination occur
once, the explicit descent which is the lovers' punishment becomes a
permanent burden or affliction. Which is to say: the myth is tragic.

It is a great theme—it can turn a good poet into a great poet. Its
grandeur and utility explain, in part, its magnetism. But the charm
doesn't always work, and many fine writers, in the grip of the narra-
tive if not the theme, are beguiled into impassioned production of dis-
appointing art. Moreover, material of this kind creates, for the writer,
a dangerous insulation, since all negative criticism can be viewed as
timidity and conservatism, terror in the presence of dark truth. But
dark truth has become unnervingly popular, a literary convention
which seems oddly incompatible with its experiential precursors: an-
guish, isolation and shame. In actual human experience, these stigmas
persist: the child who involuntarily inhabits a taboo is marked by that
fact. I don't think our society's addiction to exhibitionism and obses-

sion with progress (a narrow myth for triumph) completely explain the ease with which survivors have begun to show their wounds, making a kind of caste of isolation, competing in the previously unpermitted arena of personal shame. And the fact remains that authentic examples of transmuted suffering make plain what is missing from so many accounts.

In what would seem an impossible manoeuver, any number of poets have managed to dissociate the forbidden from all tragic implication while continuing to claim for their efforts the prestige of tragedy. The proof they offer of their authenticity is biographical accuracy. We cannot, as readers, dispute what must have been genuine suffering. The question is: why are we involved at all; what response is solicited when the documenting voice requires that we note, at all moments, its survival (even, in many cases, its survival as a soul improved by this encounter with evil). These voices specify rage and contamination and shame; what they demand, however, is admiration for unprecedented bravery, as the speaker looks back and speaks the truth. But truth of this kind will not permit itself simply to be looked back on; it makes, when it is summoned, a kind of erosion, undermining the present with the past, substituting for the shifts and approximations and variety of anecdote the immutable fixity of fate, and for curiosity regarding an unfolding future, absolute knowledge of that future. Such truth is experienced as the inescapable place and condition, not the single experience but the defining experience endlessly recreated. When the force and misery of compulsion are missing, when the scar is missing, the ambivalence which seeks, in the self, responsibility—the collusive, initiating desire which must have been present for punishment to occur, the sense that it is better, in a way, that the self be at fault than that the world be evil—when ambivalence toward the self is missing, the written recreation, no matter how artful, forfeits emotional authority.

The test for emotional authority is emotional impact, and the great flaw in Linda McCarriston's *Eva-Mary* is that, cumulatively, it isn't moving. And it is meant to be read this way, as a whole, as it is most certainly intended to move, to shock, to break the heart. One feels in these poems the delight of the ambitious artist at discovering terrain this promising: how could anything as powerful as incest fail to make devastating art?

But *Eva-Mary* is, despite its content, despite its grounding in the forbidden, despite the many wonderful individual poems, less myth than fairy tale, designed to name, localize, master and distance anxiety. I suppose if we could feel, as readers, the poignant inadequacy of the strategy, deeper response would be possible. But there seems no such signal here, no sense that this version of the past will not hold. Rather, the poems present themselves as the authentic telling of that past long suppressed, with all guilt absorbed by agents of suppression and all nobility divided among the helpless victims. It is an overt homage to the mother, and, as such, seems protected against charges of narcissistic self display. But the true object of love here is the suffering child, and the problem for artists dealing with this material is to not write from pity for the child one was but to devise a language or point of view that reinhabits anguish. *Eva-Mary* uses narrative, but its attitudes are fixed. The voice speaking suffers no dilemma toward the past, never falters in its judgments; this is a poetry, for all its artfulness, of functional simplification, and the speaker's recurring move is corrective, to be certain that, as readers, we know as clearly as she does who the heroes and villains are.

I found myself, reading this book, thinking of Forché's riveting *The Country Between Us*, which also arises out of protest, but moves deeply because it churns with self doubt as well as rage: the poems question the self's motives, expose its vanities. Unlike McCarriston's, Forché's speaker is suspect; the poems' extraordinary drama derives equally from rage at injustice (and the poems contain the additional drama of initiation into a reality of brutal unreason) and the recurring question of complicity, since it is to the poet's distinct advantage that this reality continue. Forché's willingness to sabotage the self's stature confers on the enemy an eerie humanity: can I trust what I see, the best poems suggest, given my preference to see it? When Forché falters, as she rarely does, she does so because self-doubt and self-scrutiny give way.

If I am harsh with *Eva-Mary* it is because McCarriston's obvious talent creates expectations the book fails to meet. A real gift is constantly apparent here, undermined by a narrowing agenda. What alarms is the sense of self-flattering choice, presumably the brave choice of risk and darkness, presumably the choice of the harrowingly real over the decorous artful but, in my view, the choice of the schematic over the ambivalent, complex, and truly dangerous. The poems of *Eva-Mary* resemble the pronouncements of that male judge they invoke and correct who, because he does not see, can speak in verdicts.

Forché travels to Salvador a young girl; the power of the poems has its source in her hunger to be changed, whatever the cost, to be relieved of ignorance. The self she aspires to be, the Josephine-self, is worldly, informed, brutal, direct, marked by suffering, impatient; in Forché's hierarchy of values, beauty is surpassed by wisdom; ignorance, like virginity, is something to be shed as quickly as possible, not for the novelty of the experience but because divestment—preferably scourging divestment—is the only means by which adult perspective can be achieved.

Such perspective would seem, for poets, a universal ambition, which makes recognition of its absence difficult. Sharon Olds is a poet of considerable achievement and a wholesome distaste for that most depressing of strategies, the obligatory elevation of the quotidian via mythic analogy. Olds' technique, her fascination with the extreme physical, the unsayable reality, makes a case for her presence here, and *The Father* seems, atmospherically, to draw on or suggest taboos it doesn't actually investigate. Olds has an astonishing gift for that part of the act of writing which corresponds to the hunting/gathering phase, or, to put it another way, that part which is generative: many of the poems in *The Father* read as improvisations around a single word or cluster of words, and their resourcefulness, Olds' sustained scrutiny and fastidious notation of detail, amazes. This method, which characterizes nearly every individual poem in the collection, characterizes the book as well, as though Williams' dictum regarding things had been adapted to an emotional agenda. If the book fails, as it does for me, it does so in part because the poems grow tedious: Williams' scrutiny was democratic, or perhaps, more properly, an application of the scientific method: it was a point of honor to have no bias regarding outcome. This is Williams' vitality. But Olds uses her genius for observation to make, repeatedly, the same points, to reach the same epiphanies; the energy and diversity of detail play out as stasis. The principal figures here, the speaker and her dying father, change very little; the scenes between them change very little. While we might not expect change of a dying man (his service, to the book, might be a fixity which would permit the speaker greater range in attitude and gesture as well as feeling, since response is no longer an issue), we do expect some fluidity within the speaker. What we find instead is a recalcitrant girlishness; the voice is, here, as fixed as the father, pinned to a pre-adolescent and faintly coy obsession. To some extent the drama here, father and daughter, would seem to dictate this, and the poems do recognize the problem, though their solution is not to abandon the format but to strain it: periodically, the speaker envisions the father as her child, as a fetus inside her, and so on. What the poems do not do is move either forward or backward, backward to an earlier phase of childhood, the perspectives of which might illuminate the current confrontation, or (convincingly) forward.

These issues present themselves now for two reasons. I had the good fortune to read an unpublished collection by Martha Rhodes which treats these materials (like *The Father* and *Eva-Mary*) in a booklength collection. It is difficult to give, here, adequate sense of a collection whose distinction rests in structure: Rhodes cleaves to no fixed perspective—this is a single speaker, eccentric, various, rather than a spokesperson. This fluidity persuades because it mimics the dilemma, imitates and preserves the child's helplessly reactive mind as it survives into, and is masked by, adulthood. These short poems, by turns savage, wry, mordantly witty, tender, stern, deluded, sane, read like a series of fragments, bits of mosaic; they duplicate on the page the sense of a past's being, piece by piece, recovered; they convey, devastatingly, the moment of a pattern's emerging: the little scenes and vignettes, the suspect tools of memory, cohere heart-stoppingly and absolutely into a narrative which fuses the damaged body to the divided heart. The *results* of the forbidden saturate these poems; reading them we are in the presence of harm (as we never really are in the books discussed earlier) and, simultaneously, a wild, stubborn, unkillable life. A few lines will give, perhaps, some sense of Rhodes' sad sardonic voice, and the ease with which, here, past and present blur:

She pretends to be dead
and unless you creep up and pinch her someplace tender
you think she really is dead.

Then she gets up
refreshed now, pink-cheeked,
her hair a little sweaty.

—FOR HER CHILDREN

Why do I always let you die,
not lifting you from bed, just watching you
lie breathless as your spirit
dangles from our bedroom wall
till it gives up and it's dead too.
Poof, I dream, no more you.

—OUR BEDROOM WALL

I hate to be touched, he said,
and this was news to me.

You love to be touched, I said . . .

—FOR ONCE

Back home, I'd rather not tell you where I've been.
Quietly, I take off my coat.
I open a screen, lean out and wave.
Does anyone drive slowly down our street
to stare up at our lace-lit windows?

I'm waving at parked cars, a grocery stand, the bus stop.
Here we are. Who out there
wants to be us?

—NEITHER OF US

He finds the dusty gin,
pours a double, straight,
then another. Lunch will be fast.
He'll sleep after, there,
on the sofa, I'll watch him.

It's mostly my mouth that's his,
and my hair, thinning,
pushing back from my brow, exposing
me, like him.

Oh, I've known since I was seven,
since then I've known I was him,
his.

—HIS

Secondly, I have been, for the last years, increasingly drawn to
the work of Frank Bidart, whose territory this is. The importance of
Bidart's work is difficult to overestimate; certainly he is one of the
crucial figures of our time and, very likely, a major poet—we can't, I
think, absolutely make such determinations regarding our contempo-
raries. His art, like the story of the Garden, creates narratives de-
signed to account for what would otherwise be inexplicable suffering.
Sometimes, in a kind of desperate backwards reasoning, his speakers
commit crimes, to explain or justify conditions which already exist, to
force the outward, in other words, to mirror the inward. More fier-
cely, more obsessively, more profoundly than any poet since Berry-
man (whom he in no other way resembles) Bidart explores individual
guilt, the insoluble dilemma. If Olds—at least the Olds of *The Father*—
is unintentionally static, Bidart explodes the stasis of obsession into
drama, and does so almost entirely through the resources of voice.
Anguish permeates these poems, the sense, sometimes vague, some-

times explicit, of the illicit, the criminal, and with this, the corollary issue of responsibility. Using intelligence, the single means available, these speakers struggle to trace to its source their conviction of culpability: the frantic isolation of these voices and their profound shame manifest a conviction that they are themselves reason enough for exile, whether they have acted or been acted upon. In either scenario, they are trapped. If I am responsible for evil, the poems reason, I am criminal; if I am not responsible, I am a victim and maimed. But the categories will not, in any case, stay still.

Bidart's speakers are not anomalies, strange examples of life on the edge, but a means by which the issues which absorb the poet can be most richly explored. Or perhaps less issues than conditions, the givens of human life, if human life is thought through and not merely moved through. Likewise, the evolving typographical innovations function to show multiple aspects of voice: sometimes a statement is enforced to dramatize or embody the lesson that will not stay learned, sometimes such statement seems to contain debate, as though the true force of statement were question: not "I did it" but "Did I? Did I?", a disguised plea for corroboration, the testing of a statement's truth by way of its sound. But corroboration, except of a particular kind I'll discuss shortly, is impossible, in part because these speakers' failure to resolve fundamental questions regarding themselves paralyzes their capacity to judge, or trust, the outside world (in other words, they cannot trust their impressions because they have not identified their purposes) and partly because compulsive conviction of the self's guilt tends to diminish the reality of an outside world which does not, in sufficient intensity, acknowledge that guilt. What Bidart's speakers share is a terminal dependence on intelligence, and minimal relief of accuracy: ". . . insight like ashes: clung/ to; useless; hated." Nothing, in these poems, is simple.

Nor is there any plausible relief. Love and passion are rare here; when they occur, they show their secret, their clandestine aspect. The only invitation eros can imagine, the only absolute available to humanity, is the creation of a non-thing, an erasure, a wound, the inflicting of damage that will not heal:

> ". . . . You said
> that the dead
>
> rule and confuse our steps—
> that if I helped you cut your skin
> deeply enough
>
> that, at least, was IRREPARABLE . . .'"

The ambition of passion is to replicate the drama of Eden. Or, that drama was invented to explain the drive of two beings toward an animal pact of shared isolation, the drive to make of the body a souvenir or proof of the event.

Virtually any poem in Bidart's *In the Western Night* can stand as a paradigm; virtually any poem shocks in a way that McCarriston and Olds never do. In "Confessional" particularly, the power of the forbidden to take two hostages shows in a sustained bravura feat of disclosure. This is passion at work, with passion's drive toward the irreparable:

> "she began to simplify her life, denied
> herself, and said that she and I must struggle
>
> "to divest ourselves
> of the love of CREATED BEINGS,"—
>
> and to help me to do that,
> one day
>
>   she hanged my cat."

The poem, like many of Bidart's, begins and ends in bondage, the smaller bondage of individual life contained within the larger bondage of the species, the first (apparently) caused by, cemented by, the cat's death, the second the *reason* for that death. The voice that speaks in "Confessional" is the child, the done-unto, the passive watcher, the victim; he is haunted by his mother's act because it represents his own culpability; he participates with his mother in its creation. The space in which the speaker lives with his mother is a sealed space, characterized by exclusion, intimacy, that quality of deadlock which exactly renders the condition of victimization, its conviction of its own agency, its will toward responsibility. And the guilt which gives "Confessional" its title and situation is the guilt of collusion which arises out of or creates the forbidden: not that the act of violence is specifically sought or arranged by the victim, but that its enactment binds victim to perpetrator in a pact of silence. It is the silence that is collusive, that becomes for the victim the emblem of his or her deepest relation, since only with the one who damaged him are there no secrets. And the progressive effect of such conspiracy is the gradual diminishment of all other possibility, the retreat of other voices, until, in this instance, mother and son are entirely and absolutely alone, entirely enmeshed, dependent on one another for authentication:

". . . . how can I talk about

the way in which, when I was young,

we seemed to be engaged in an ENTERPRISE
together,—

      the enterprise of "figuring out the world,"
figuring out her life, my life,—

THE MAKING OF HER SOUL,

        which somehow, in our "enterprise"
together, was the making of my soul,—"

"Confessional" searches wildly for historical analogy because insight affords insufficient possibility of change. But change, for Bidart, is specious; it gives lie to the overwhelming seriousness of, the reality of, his perception. These poems do not triumph over damage and shame, they find no cure, no respite, but, in the manner of the great tragedies, Bidart's voices protest (as Edmond White has observed). And the gravity of our dilemma, in being so profoundly experienced, in being given durable form, is dignified.

There are other modes than the tragic; plainly neither McCarriston not Olds intended to sound exactly this note. And one of the revelations of art is the discovery of a tone or perspective at once wholly unexpected and wholly true to a set of materials. The problem in both *Eva-Mary* and *The Father* isn't the refusal of the tragic vision but the failure of both authors to find alternative visions. *Eva-Mary* is limited by McCarriston's managerial interventions, her insistence on a single rigid interpretation; limited, in a sense, by excess will. Whereas *The Father* suffers from an insufficiency of will or direction; the poems are nearly all better in their parts than as wholes, as is the collection. The aimlessness of the book itself suggests the single disadvantage of Olds' impressive facility: these poems read as great talent with, at the moment, nowhere to go. Neither of these conditions need determine these poets' futures. But I find myself concerned that, in their different ways, McCarriston and Olds are constrained by a like mechanism, the felt obligation of the woman writer to give encouraging voice to the life force (for want of a better term).

Because the character of the voice, in each case, is intended to be expansive, non-judgmental, rooted in the physical, intended to be the heroic voice of the survivor, one doesn't automatically associate its production with constriction. But to the poet, all obligation of this kind is constriction, and ought to be questioned or fought.

OBSTINATE HUMANITY

Robinson Jeffers appears to be a poet other poets chastize eloquently. That is: the inducement to literary reprimand is in proportion to the stakes: the grander, the more fundamental the objection, the more inviting the project. The remarkable poems of this little genre, Milosz's and Hass's, are devoid of flamboyant condescension, at least insofar as the living can avoid flaunting their ongoing development at the immobile dead. "So brave in a void/ you offered sacrifices to demons": so Milosz addresses Jeffers. If not exactly tribute, this is nevertheless a particular species of reproach: giant to giant.

The reprimand is moral: at issue is humanity, the definition thereof. And Jeffers' crime, in Milosz's poem, "to proclaim . . . an inhuman thing." Hass concurs, pretty much, though his formulation changes the emphasis, focusing on causes: "human anguish made him cold."

What's odd to me is that Jeffers in all his hardness and obstinate fixity and dogmatic revulsions is, of the three, the most poignantly, albeit cheerlessly, human.

I read Milosz in translation, which makes discussion of tone problematic. And yet, at issue in his poem to Jeffers is the placement of the speaker relative to his subjects and, in fact, Milosz speaks as a diplomat, an envoy, his mission being to explain, or represent, one form of paganism to another.

The paganism he defends is maternal. Earth centered. Moon centered. Fruitful. Predictable. Cyclical. This is the same fecund earth Hass reveres. Both approve it as the wise man approves woman, radiant in otherness. Homage to the source, the root, but homage paid, in Milosz, by someone well beyond primitive gesturing.

The mathematical equivalent of feminine earth is multiplication: increase, whatever its metaphoric manifestation, seems inherently life-affirming. Whereas the corresponding, the declared metaphor for Jeffers' earth, the "massive mysticism of stone," is elimination: a dead end, presumably.

Hass puts all this more eloquently: "though rock stands it does not breed." He sees the lure of rock but names its spiritual danger: sterility. To stand, to not breed, is to be finally inhuman, and, pragmatically, *not* lasting: the future of the species is more profitably assured through reproduction than through endurance. In Hass's mind, mutability, not fixity, sponsors ongoing existence. And yet the manner in which Jeffers espouses rock is immensely human: exposed, rash, extreme, vulnerable. Rigid, where Hass and Milosz are lithe-minded, evolved.

Jeffers writes out of enraged, disappointed romanticism: civilized in his expectations, he cannot forgive civilization in that it wasn't worth his faith. This can seem, to a reader, cumulatively trying: repetition deprives a last stand of its dramatic force.

Whereas Hass characteristically resists resolution: a mark of intellect, but also a temperamental inclination which can creates its own form of stasis, in that it lacks not motion but momentum.

Hass hates disappointment, hates being imprisoned in its continuing and limited range of attitudes, of tones: rue, regret, plangent lament. When Hass *sighs* in *Praise* he does so with a kind of savage fury, constrained by perspective, by habitual poise; in these moments, he comes closest to being what Milosz has always been, since to write as an ancient soul is to write as an ironist (the alternative, I suppose, being to sing the purest and briefest of lyrics—).

Hass's method of poetic development has always been exposure: he uses his empathetic capacity to extend his range. Though he is not, I think, at home in irony (unless there is irony in the Buddha's composure), he has most certainly, as Milosz's translator, been exposed to its most subtle and resourceful practitioner.

Hass and Milosz have in common astounding intellectual gifts and the virtuoso's mastery of tone which contrives to endow natural speech with a sometimes unbelievable subtext of resonances. But the sources of flexibility differ: Milosz's detachment differs from Hass's empathy, as irony is distinct from ambivalence.

It will be interesting to see whether Hass ripens into the sort of poet Milosz is: ironic, but with an irony by turns delicate, malicious, passionate, judgmental, tender. He already has Milosz's 360-degree gaze, as opposed to Jeffers' fixity.

Jeffers' ferocity is alien to Hass; his landscapes less so. Like Jeffers, Hass is attracted to the absence of the human. There have been, from the first, counterparts in Hass to Jeffers' harsh, unpopulated world. And this is an aspect of the work even in *Field Guide*, even before human presence or human agency come to be characterized as that contaminating "steady thoughtlessness." But where Jeffers' imagination settles on rock and hawk, Hass gives us frog and pond, a bowl of oranges. Into these worlds, human beings, men and women, come as intrusions.

Most poets are, in Frost's phrase, acquainted with the night. Hass is unique in having inhabited, as an adult, a sunlit world. Exiled from Eden, he's like the man who's always been healthy and gets sick: when the amazement passes, he simply can't stand feeling this way. And the tonal problem of *Praise*, the collection that registers this change, is to avoid petulant irritability.

The earlier work, "The Return of Robinson Jeffers," is built around a move typical of Hass's work, early and late, an extended enactment of empathy. Hass imagines Jeffers' return from death: "I imagine him thinking . . . ": so the meditation starts. Hass's projected epiphany duplicates Milosz's bias; this is not curious, since they address the same figure, the same perceived limitation. Jeffers, in Hass's imagination, " . . . feels pain as rounding at the hips, as breasts." And the form reeducation takes is the birth of feminine empathy and suffering to replace male arrogance.

It is either very touching, very feminine (on this grid) or extremely arrogant that Hass prefers to imagine these revelations as occurring to Jeffers himself, while at the same time refusing to abandon his own position as narrating, as sponsoring intelligence: the epiphany occurs in Hass's imagination. The fact is, Hass has learned much from Jeffers. There are tastes in common: the long, rhythmic, complicated sentences, with subsequent sentences beginning on a repeated phrase, like a thread picked up in a complex tapestry, so that one is always aware of, always hearing the human voice (the danger of complex syntax being that voice will be lost and, with it, intimacy, directness). The similarities are, in any case, easy to hear, for all the difference in ambiance: " . . . . what a festival for the seafowl./ What a witches' sabbath of wings/ Hides the water." That's Jeffers, but Hass has moments very like.

What Hass does, what no one else now writing does with such skill, is a kind of spiritual ventriloquism: he is able to project not merely voice but a whole sensibility. On the surface, this resembles Keats's ideas of negative capability; in fact, it differs profoundly from Keats, in motive and effect. Always Keats's excursions conclude, and the act of conclusion marks a restoration of self. This is the romantic journey: it might be, it can be imagined, it is not. Hass may assert the fact of limitation, but limitation does not seem to be an attribute of the voice. And the romantic sound is not one Hass seems especially eager to make. His poems are, regularly, a flight from self; what they lack, when they lack anything, is a sense of the restrictions of self, of singleness, which perception necessitates acts of judgment, decision, assertion of priorities. His poems repudiate self in its romantic role: bedrock, shaping principle.

It is appropriate that Jeffers attracts moral criticism: he is himself, in the manner of the darker prophets, obsessed with morality. At stake is the salvation of the race. Always he hungers after large simplicities: "Why does insanity always twist the great answers?/ Because only/ tormented persons want the truth."

As for mankind in general: "Truly men hate the truth; they'd liefer/ Meet a tiger in the road." He built into his poems the romance of not being listened to. He wanted not to be coddled; often, he seems to try to see humankind without human bias, aspiring not to the communal "cordiality and affection" but to the isolated falcon's "Realistic eyes and act."

The "act," for the artist, was not simply to see, but also to judge. The aesthetic that refuses judgment forfeits, for Jeffers, moral density. Thus the Chinese anthology: "These men were better/ Artists than any of ours, and far better observers. They loved landscape/ And put man in his place. But why/ Do their rocks have no weight? They loved rice-wine and peace and friendship,/ Above all they loved landscape and solitude,/ —like Wordsworth. But Wordsworth's mountains have weight and mass, dull though the song be."

The Chinese poets share certain of Jeffers' biases, but they refuse to substitute speculations on the eternal for fastidious notation of the temporal. If, for Jeffers, they do not satisfy, at least they do not commit the more dangerous errors of self-delusion which occur primarily in the moral or spiritual spheres. As both reader and writer, Jeffers wants what "only tormented persons want"; he is correspondingly suspicious of comfort, of the distractions of pleasure. He despises those spiritual or ethical systems which encourage self-forgiveness; it may be this adamant horror of mercy to which Milosz particularly objects.

The anthropomorphic impulse which, in his address to Jeffers, Milosz commends produces life-enhancing miracles which seem the substance, or confirmation, of "grace and hope"; it is this impulse that makes domestic realities potentially the site of the divine: "Then, under the apple trees/ Angels in homespun linen will come parting the boughs . . ." So ravishingly tender is the image as to make one forget that human culture is not, in fact, so wholly benign. But Jeffers' struggle has been to see the sun without an intervening image, not as a "farmer's ruddy face"; his vanity is to believe in the possibility. Jeffers' poems do not "implore protection"—to be protected is to not see, and Jeffers makes a cult of exposure—even as they regularly confess helplessness, despair. Jeffers wants to see the world with a gaze approximating the falcon's "realistic" one; what Jeffers calls "realistic" Milosz sees as "inhuman."

"No one with impunity/ gives himself the eyes of a god," Milosz says. Clarity is not within human capability. And yet the preference for clarity over solace and the striving toward it is, in Jeffers, both moving and honorable. If Jeffers was brave "in a void" it was in part because he rejected the conditions of the "white kolkhoz tablecloth": his vanity was his vision of himself in relation to a single truth, but there are other and dangerous vanities, intolerances: the tribe's automatic allegiance to itself, for example. "Cordiality and affection" exclude those who do not participate in the social contract.

Jeffers lived in a terrifying time; it was not his nature to seek tolerable arrangements despite the world's state. Nor could he pray to the available projections; he did not find the world better for its religions. For Jeffers, the central fact of the founders of these religions is their inflamed humanity:

Here was a man who was born a bastard, and among the people
That more than any in the world valued race-purity, chastity,
    the prophetic splendors of the race of David.
Oh intolerable wound, dimly perceived. Too loving to curse his
    mother, desert driven, devil haunted,
The beautiful young poet found truth in the desert, but found also
Fantastic solution of hopeless anguish. The carpenter was not
    his father? Because God was his father,
Not a man sinning, but the pure holiness and power of God.
    His personal anguish and insane solution
Have stained an age; nearly two thousand years are one vast
    poem drunk with the wine of his blood.

In his stubborn, desperate way, Jeffers sought a plausible and sustaining vision, sought it explicitly outside the human circle, but sought it with an unremittingly human yearning. He wanted to find something in the world which was not corrupt, not the product of corruption:

I think, here is your emblem
To hang in the future sky;
Not the cross, not the hive,

But this; bright power, dark peace;
Fierce consciousness joined with final
Disinterestedness;

Life with calm death; the falcon's
Realistic eyes and act
Married to the massive

Mysticism of stone,
Which failure cannot cast down
Nor success make proud.

DISRUPTION,
HESITATION,
SILENCE

In my generation, most of the poets I admire are interested in length: they want to write long lines, long stanzas, long poems, poems which cover an extended sequence of events. To all this I feel an instant objection, whose sources I'm not confident I know. Some of the sources may lie in character, in my tendency to reject all ideas I didn't think of first, which habit creates a highly charged adversarial relationship with the new. What is positive in this process is that it creates an obligation to articulate an argument.

What I share with my friends is ambition; what I dispute is its definition. I do not think that more information always makes a richer poem. I am attracted to ellipsis, to the unsaid, to suggestion, to eloquent, deliberate silence. The unsaid, for me, exerts great power: often I wish an entire poem could be made in this vocabulary. It is analogous to the unseen; for example, to the power of ruins, to works of art either damaged or incomplete. Such works inevitably allude to larger contexts; they haunt because they are not whole, though wholeness is implied: another time, a world in which they were whole, or were to have been whole, is implied. There is no moment in which their first home is felt to be the museum. A few years ago, I saw a show of Holbein drawings; most astonishing were those still in progress. Parts were entirely finished. And parts were sketched, a fluent line indicating arm or hand or hair, but the forms were not filled in. Holbein had made notes to himself: this sleeve blue, hair, auburn. The terms were other—not the color in the world, but the color in paint or chalk. What these unfinished drawings generated was a vivid sense of Holbein at work, at the sitting; to see them was to have a sense of being back in time, back in the middle of something. Certain works of art become artifacts. By works of art, I mean works in any medium. And certain works of art do not. It seems to me that what is wanted, in art, is to harness the power of the unfinished. All earthly experience is partial. Not simply because it is subjective, but because that which we do not know, of the universe, of mortality, is so much more vast than that which we do know. What is unfinished or has been destroyed participates in these mysteries. The problem is to make a whole that does not forfeit this power.

The argument for completion, for thoroughness, for exhaustive detail, is that it makes an art more potent because more exact—a closer recreation of the real. But the cult of exhaustive detail, of data, needs scrutiny. News stories are detailed. But they don't seem, at least to me, at all real. Their thoroughness is a reprimand to imagination; and yet they don't say this is what it was to be here.

I belong, so it appears, to a generation suspicious of the lyric, of brevity, of the deception of stopped time. And impatient with beauty, which is felt to be an inducement to stupor. Certainly there is stupor everywhere; it is an obvious byproduct of anxiety. But narrative poetry, or poetry packed with information, is not the single escape from the perceived constrictions of the lyric. A number of quite different writers practice in various ways another method.

No one seems particularly to want to define the lyric. Donald Hall provides a definition which he immediately repudiates as being too general to be useful. Louis Simpson says the lyric poem is any poem expressing personal emotion rather than describing events. The opposite, in other words, of the news story. The expression of personal emotions depends, obviously, on the existence of a voice, a source of emotion. The lyric is, traditionally, intense, traditionally, also, "a moment's thought." Though it is foolish to attempt a close reading of a poem in a language one doesn't know, I want, briefly, to talk about Rilke's "Archaic Torso of Apollo" in that it is a magnificent example of lyric poetry and, as well, structurally remarkable: its last line anticipates the technique I mean to talk about.

Anticipates only because to shift terms at the end explodes a boundary but does not create, within the poem, that space which is potentially an alternative to information.

"We cannot know," Rilke says of the torso of Apollo. The unknowable is the poem's first referent, the context. And it is interesting to try to imagine the poem's arising out of another, a whole, statue. Something is lost; the poem turns a little corny, a little trite. For something whole, the act of giving directions is simple bossiness, nor is any virtuosity involved in the act of hearing such directions. What wholeness gives up is the dynamic: the mind need not rush in to fill a void. And Rilke loved his voids. In the broken thing, moreover, human agency is oddly implied: breakage, whatever its cause, is the dark complement to the act of making; the one implies the other. The thing that is broken has particular authority over the act of change.

Rilke's poem begins with the unknowable, a void located in the past. And ends with the unknown: a new, a different, life; a void projected into the future. But the impression the poem gives is no more symmetrical than is the statue: the force of the imperative is abrupt, like breakage; the swerving assaults us, implicates, challenges.

Rilke's greatness, for me, is in the making of poems which marry lyric intensity to irregularity of form. Neither Berryman nor Oppen nor Eliot seems to me much like Rilke. Yet each is, in some way, a master of not saying.

Which seems a very odd way to think of Berryman, with his high excitability and multiple personalities. A colleague of mine at Williams, Anita Sokolsky, used the word *distractedness* to describe a

primary attribute of *The Dream Songs*. I like the way the word calls up
a sense of bewilderedness, of childishness: in his behaviors, if not in
the breadth of his suffering, Henry Pussycat is very much the preco-
cious child, the child with the short attention span, the child keenly
aware of audience.

Implicit in the idea of the lyric is the single voice: Berryman's
primary disruption of the lyric is the fracturing of voice. From poem
to poem, the paradigm varies: minstrel show, schizophrenia, psycho-
analysis. But always one persona taking over for another, taking
the stage: these are noisy poems—shattered, voluble, fragmented,
desperate, dramatic, futile. The intense purpose characteristic of the
lyric becomes, in Berryman, intense cross-purposes. In other words,
paralysis.

The first Dream Song is as good an example as any. The poem
begins with two lines of report: our speaker is someone who knows
Henry from the outside ("huffy" being descriptive of behavior) and
from the inside ("unappeasable"). Reasonable, then, to presume that
the central figure—with a curious detachment that contains the inter-
nalized perpetual reproach of a parent—here describes himself. And
reasonable, too, to anticipate consistency, if not of tone, certainly of
perspective. But reason is not the long suit of dreams. If Henry, in
lines one and two, is the speaker, the guiding or prevailing intelli-
gence, then who is the "I" of line three? Friendly to the cause, adult,
capable of entertaining several ideas at once ("his point" suggests the
many other angles already considered). A reader encountering the
first person tends to identify that pronoun with a poem's central in-
telligence. But the problem in *The Dream Songs*, the drama of the
poems, is the absence of a firm self. The proliferating selves dramatize,
they do not disguise, this absence. It is interesting, on this point, to
think of Hopkins, who is in so many ways Berryman's antecedent.
The sound of Berryman is like the sound of Hopkins; both poets are
animated by self-disgust. But self, in Hopkins, is a miserable fixity, a
pole remote from God. God is other, distant, visible in flashes,
abidingly present in the world. In Berryman, there is no such sense

of abiding presence. What in Hopkins are two separated halves, agonized self and remote God, are in Berryman conflated. This would seem an advantage, but is not. Hopkins was permitted reverence. The very remoteness of God, the felt division between God and self, which could become a metaphor for the division between pure good and pure evil, allowed for, perpetuated belief in, good. This separation encouraged those beliefs which support life: belief in virtue, belief in the world's essential beauty and order, belief in God's superior and embracing wisdom. There is no such reliable other in Berryman. There is no you because there is no I; no fundamental self. The stable, if anguished, relation between man and God in Hopkins has no parallel in Berryman, at least in *The Dream Songs.*

Meanwhile, in the poem, an "I" has made its debut. The ruminative tone of the third line suggests that its commentary may go on. In fact, it doesn't: the "I" is immediately absorbed into the intimate, childish rancors of lines four and five. "Do it" means *do to:* it is all things done to Henry against Henry's unknown, unknowable best interests. The very idea, which is actually Henry's, that others have such power is enough to send Henry into violent hiding. The power is vague because its agents are hazy. What exists is a sense of victimization, of jeopardy, but it is never particularly explicit. In fact, so well does Henry hide himself that, ultimately, he can't find where he is either. And the self that's hidden wakes occasionally, as in number 29, trying to account for its condition: "But never did Henry, as he thought he did,/end anyone and hack her body up/and hide the pieces, where they may be found." He looks for a crime to account for feelings: he behaves like a criminal, like someone in flight. Guilt explains flight. But so, too, does an ancient wish to protect a very fragile self.

The endless compensatory coming out and talking of *The Dream Songs* cannot change the character so formed. The last line of the first stanza is the line of fate: he should have. He didn't. Spoken by the mother, her head shaking sadly.

In terms of method, the next stanzas go on in much the same

way. But there's a surprising turn in stanza three, surprising and heartbreaking. Who says "Once in a sycamore I was glad/all at the top, and I sang"? This is an "I" different from the "I" of stanza one, who sees, or the "I" of stanza two, who doesn't see. This is engagement, not commentary. This is a whole being, in behavior spontaneous, Henry-like, but in tone, calm. The Dream Songs search for such wholeness. But Berryman's genius, unlike Rilke's, is not expressed as longing.

The Dream Songs are quilts, collages. One way to read them is to insist on coherence, to elaborate the associative process, to pay too little attention to the gaps, the juxtapositions. We can supply what's missing, but the electricity of the poetry derives from Berryman's refusal to narrate these transformations.

Berryman at his worst, raves. No poet seems farther from that act than George Oppen. And for all the brilliant sleight of hand, for all the wit and bravura, for all the savage intelligence, the undernote of Berryman is pathos ranging to grief. The background is the abyss; the poems venture as close to the edge as possible. To some extent, this was inescapable, to some extent cultivated. In his magnificent essay on Anne Frank, Berryman writes, "We have been tracing a psychological and moral development to which, if I am right, no close parallel can be found. It took place under very special circumstances, which—let us now conclude, as she concluded—though superficially unfavorable, [were] in fact highly favorable to it; she was forced to mature, in order to survive; the hardest challenge, let's say, that a person can face without defeat is the best for him." This is noble justification as well as stunning analysis, brilliant and lucid like all the essays. Berryman, in any case, admired extreme states; control interested him very little.

It is valuable, though nearly impossible, to try to read Oppen and Berryman side by side. Nothing in Oppen feels involuntary. And yet nothing feels rigid. One impression genius fosters is that there is, beside it, no comparable mastery: no other way to sound, to think, to be. I admire both Berryman and Oppen to this degree; I regret not knowing what these two thought of each other. Berryman's meticulous need to offend everyone, to be certain that in no mind was he even briefly associated with anything even slightly conservative, mannerly, acceptable, his poignant but extremely wily egotism sometimes seems childish and limited beside Oppen. And sometimes, next to Berryman's feverish wildness, Oppen seems too lofty, too hermetic, too secure. Temperamentally, they seem to cancel one another out. And yet, like Berryman, Oppen is a master of juxtaposition. Interruption seems the wrong term; there is nothing of distractedness or disorientation in this work. Berryman's *Dream Songs* project shatteredness; Oppen's poetry, to my mind, demonstrates its opposite: a profound integrity, a self so well established, so whole, as to be invisible.

Surprisingly, Oppen's clean, austere, dynamic poetry has very few active verbs. No one uses the verb of being better—in these poems, it gives observation the aura and resonance of truth. What moves these poems is silence; in structural terms, Oppen's pauses correspond to Berryman's distractions. "Street" begins with a sighed demonstrative. There is no surprise, no histrionic excitement:

STREET

Ah these are the poor,
These are the poor—

Bergen street.

Humiliation,
Hardship . . .

Nor are they very good to each other;
It is not that. I want

An end of poverty
As much as anyone

For the sake of intelligence,
'The conquest of existence'—

It has been said, and is true

And this is real pain,
Moreover. It is terrible to see the children,

The righteous little girls;
So good, they expect to be so good. . . .

One is obliged, here, to acquiesce to what is factually present: moral-
ity, for Oppen, begins in clarity, and it is the latter which can be culti-
vated. Repetition prolongs the moment and threatens, briefly, to
create its own, and false, order. But the dash propels the poem. A
period, grammatically, would have done. But a period doesn't force
motion, and part of Oppen's genius is a reluctance to conclude. His
poems need this reluctance, need his suspicion of closure, in that their
manner of expression is absolute.

Only one line in this poem has the force of the double stop: no
enjambment, no propulsive punctuation:/"Bergen street." A recall to
the specific which, in its terseness, takes on the finality of diagnosis.
So final does the line seem as to make it difficult, for me, in any case,
to see how the poem was even resumed. The silence that measures in-
tervals is, in Oppen, the time it takes for information to be absorbed:
there is almost never an analogous process in Berryman, as there is
nothing in Oppen which resembles Berryman's aggressive parrying.
Bergen street. Silence. Then the available generalizations. But these
are so arranged as to construct a parallel: they follow in a vertical line
after the named place so that they become, in a sense, synonyms for
Bergen Street. And after the generalizations, the ruminative ellipsis.
The ensuing pause contains a suppressed assertion: the poem actively
resumes with a denial. This is a characteristic move in Oppen, the
idea implied in being dismissed. And now, in the poem, personal re-
sponse is volunteered, but the feelings of the "I" are the feelings of
anyone: personal distinction is not claimed. Nor is conventional feel-
ing held in bland contempt: reasonable, the poem suggests, to despise
poverty.

One of the interesting things about this poem is the fact that, to
this point, very little of the language is vivid. The poem exists in tim-

ing, in the way ideas are held in suspension, so that, by the end, what is charged becomes indisputable in context of such plainness. This is a poetry of mind, of mind processing information—not a mind incapable of response but a mind wary of premature response; a mind, that is, not hungering after sensation. I find, in Oppen, a sanity so profound as to be mysterious: this is a sound that has, for the most part, disappeared from poetry, possibly from thought.

The poem moves as a unit from the semi-colon in line six to the dash in line eleven; typical of the absorbing mind is "it has been said, and is true." But the true is not a resting place, not an epiphany. Or: this truth is not. It is incidental: the maxim is passive, the street relentless. Oppen has, in the most literal sense, an open mind, a mind resistant to closure. What is so rare in him is not that, but the simultaneous austerity and distaste for blather.

The poem refuses to project its informing intelligence. The figures beheld remain themselves, and apart. This is not insufficiency of feeling, but absence of vanity. Pain belongs, here, properly to the children, not the speaker. It may be terrible to see the children, but it is far more terrible to be the children. The speaker's detachment is his, and our, particular burden. Like someone watching *Agamemnon,* he knows what will happen. Oppen brings to what he sees integrity of two kinds: personal wholeness and probity of intent. His poem is not a campaign; he does not propose himself as the missing advocate or champion of the little girls. Whatever he does, in life, on their behalf, is not alluded to in the poem. The poem honors a boundary: the boundary of Bergen Street, the difference between the circumstances of its natives and the circumstances of the visitor. The boundary, in absolute terms, between one being and another. Bad enough for those little girls: at least let the poem not appropriate their experience.

The resources of the poem are given over to characterization of the observed: in a work so nearly devoid of modifiers, "righteous" is galvanizing. What follows is, in its repetition, parallel to the poem's first lines: a translation, a refinement, a correction. And the poem itself becomes an act of wrenching sympathy.

Oppen regularly defines things by saying what they are not. This method of creation through eradication is, for me, congenial. And I find it helpful, in trying to analyze his poetry, to say what it isn't, or what it does not do. Conspicuously, it does not impose. As the speaker's relation to the children is devoid of proprietary impulses, so that the poem seems, ultimately, to dignify the little girls, to pay homage, similarly, in relation to the reader, the poem is neither didactic nor overbearing. It is rare, almost, in my experience, peculiar to Oppen, to find such tact in combination with such intensity.

In most writing, talk is energy and stillness its opposite. But Oppen's pauses are dense with argument: they actively further the poem. When poems are difficult, it is often because their silences are complicated, hard to follow. For me, the answer to such moments is not more language.

What I am advocating is, of course, the opposite of Keats's dream of filling rifts with ore. The dream of abundance does not need another defense. The danger of that aesthetic is its tendency to produce, in lesser hands, work that is all detail and no shape. Meanwhile, economy is not admired. Economy depends on systematic withholding of the gratuitous; dispute is bound to arise over definitions of "gratuitous," but the very action of withholding is currently suspect. It is associated with rigidity, miserliness, insufficiencies; with faculties either atrophied or checked. It is a habit not admired in personal interaction, in which realm it is associated with ideas of manipulation, slyness, coldness; it is considered uniformly dangerous in governments, and so on.

The art of George Oppen is bold, severe, mysterious, intense, serene and fiercely economical. The advantage of the last, in my view, is that it promotes depth. Each turn is distilled, each movement essential. What would take the more expansive poet ten lines, Oppen does in two. That fact alone forces him to go on. Whereas the expansive poet is prone to premature linguistic satiation, by which I mean that the sense of something's having been made comes into existence too readily. The ratio of words to meaning favors words. The poem exists in its adornments. But no poem of Oppen's can be further reduced than it has already been by its maker. This means that the time it takes, as thought, is the time it requires, not the time the writer requires.

The ambitions of economy are deeply bound to the idea of form. And form, in this connection, usually appears as a chaste thing. Eliot writes:

> Words, after speech, reach
> Into the silence. Only by the form, the pattern
> Can words or music reach
> The stillness, as a Chinese jar still
> Moves perpetually in its stillness.

This is late Eliot, but the dominant themes are present from the very first.

When, in "The Love Song of J. Alfred Prufrock," Prufrock asks, "Is it perfume from a dress/ That makes me so digress?" the question is, itself, a kind of ruse. "Digress" suggests that some purposeful journey has been interrupted. "To stray," says the dictionary, "from the main subject." The word introduces an idea that has not, it seems, been actually present to the poem: the idea of a main subject.

"The Love Song of J. Alfred Prufrock" is a poem of pathological delay. The action of the poem is inaction, stalling. "Let us go, then, you and I,/ When the evening is spread out against the sky." But Prufrock puts off starting: the second line suggests that the time proper to going, though imminent, hasn't arrived. The verbs of the poem describe an arc; they approximate an action. Let us go; there will be; I have known; how should I; would it have been—and then, dramatically, the present tense: I grow old, followed by the alternating future and past perfect. But nothing, in fact, occurs; nothing is even begun. Prufrock fears action; the poem specifically dramatizes, in its formidable hesitations, a fear of beginnings.

The poem, it is true, puts forth explanations: the casual, contemptuous dismissal of the lady, for example. But these seem screens, constructed to account for a pre-existing terror. The future is impossible, the past lost. And the present a vacuum: non-action. Simply, I grow old. The refusal to take action, the permanent hesitation of standing still, has not, unfortunately, the desired effect: time does not stop.

Time is Prufrock's enemy, and Eliot's recurring subject. Time is that which mocks the idea of eternity, the stillness of the Chinese jar, a state of positive, dynamic non-change. In time, nothing achieves this stillness; nothing is incapable of being reversed. To another nature, this very fact would be an inducement to action, but long-meditated action wants to leave a mark. Indeed, it hardly matters, as Prufrock irately notes, to ask, of the overwhelming question: what is it? In a universe in which everything is in flux, nothing is final, and, to Prufrock, the authority of "overwhelming" depends on finality. Why suffer for anything less?

To begin, here, is to presume. The words recur and finally merge as the poem's agony intensifies. "Presume" is Prufrock's motif, with its suggestion of social error, of brute, clumsy will imposing itself. To venture, to dare, to take liberties. And, as well, to take on faith. To begin, you must believe in a future; motion enacts that belief. Prufrock stands to one side, out of the way of savage time, but changed anyway. The poem is all wringing of hands, its rhymes regularly sealing off options. Prufrock, in being motionless, does his best imitation of being inert: " . . . that which is only living/ Can only die."

Eliot has written the masterpiece of avoidance. At the poem's center is the unsaid, the overwhelming question, the moment forced to its crisis. But Prufrock is not Lazarus; he does not tell all.

This is a dramatic poem. And the pathos of Prufrock is a subject separate from the greatness of this achievement. The poem is satire not in that Prufrock is mistaken, but in that he is inadequate to the discipline of contemplation: we can hear, almost, the very young poet cautioning himself. As a dramatic poem, the whole would dissolve were the overwhelming question elaborated. "It is impossible to say just what I mean!" This bursts from Prufrock, at a moment of frustration. But the underlying tension recurs throughout the oeuvre.

A danger of the expansive poem is that this tension is lost. Not all the poets I've talked about write specifically of this struggle. Certainly, no such strain shows in Oppen. And yet in each case some element of conquest remains, a sense of the importance of exact language, a sense of being in the presence of the crucial. There are poets I love whose work suggests infinite ease, but even in such poets, the best poems often turn on or evolve out of a misperception, something too easily seen or too readily said. Not every temperament inclines to elaboration. What I've said has been meant not to eliminate a method but to speak for the virtues of a style which inclines to the suggested over the amplified.

DISINTERESTEDNESS

The essay that means to defend disinterestedness by claiming it exists will be both very short and very weak; even the essay on perfect goodness would be longer. Further, triumphant announcement by a generation of readers that impartiality, the absence of what my dictionary calls "selfish bias", cannot inform the act of reading distracts from a more pragmatic debate concerning the implications of an ideal, which is what disinterestedness—reading as though one had no personality—must be.

The function of an ideal is to compel, in our behavior, its approximation. Thus the fantasy of perfect goodness and craving toward it inspire individual acts of goodness (also, possibly, rebellious acts of violence, the furious objection to the impossible standard). I believe that the attempt to read disinterestedly encourages that reading which best apprehends the page and most passionately registered whatever is held there. Self interest is speaking: through this means, more accrues to the reader. Even the historical eye of criticism is served, since no account *in medias* can more tellingly dramatize the ambiance of a period than the attempt to omit the self from description. Inevitably, in any reading, some aspect of the work at hand will be emphasized or avoided; when these readings occur systematically, in the scrutiny of literature by various minds, the preoccupations and beliefs of an epoch declare themselves. Our present avidity to publish our biases, to introduce them into analysis, seems like skittishness— no one is going to do to us what we do to our predecessors. We are obsessed with exposure, and prefer to take the initiative, to expose ourselves.

All this describes receptivity, which begins with the self's efface-ment. This we fear in ourselves because we link passivity to non-existence and fear in others, perceiving a danger to ourselves in receptivity's acquisitive capaciousness. But the analogy between hu-man relations and the relation of reader to page is false: it ignores the fundamental distinction between willed self-effacement, which is temporary, and helpless self-effacement, which is annihilation.

Granted the self without "selfish bias" doesn't exist, suspending, a little longer, discussion of advantage, the practical question remains: how does an actual self approach a work of literature imitating the paradigm? Insofar as possible, by enacting the pretense: at issue is not what the mind is but how it conducts itself. So, for the moment, it suspends opinion and response, all the means by which it has so long struggled to define itself, attempting, instead, neutrality, attentive-ness; for the moment, it plays dead; only a very deep confidence in lit-erature's power allows this, and only the training in pretense allows the birth of such confidence. The hope of animation through the work of art infuses this manner of reading with a constant ongoing anticipatory energy; as the work is absorbed, the idling mind responds with checked gratitude. Checked lest gratitude give too premature a report of itself and, in so doing, forfeit some part of the inexhausted work.

What is omitted from this approach is the notion of dialogue: the forceful self engaging the shifting work. For the calculated pa-tience of disinterest, such cooperative reading substitutes dispute, de-bate, challenge alternating with enthusiastic accord. The superficial fluidity and dynamism of this method mask its deeper rigidity and limitedness. Also its cumulative dreariness: the imposition of one's own personality on a work, for all the momentary giddiness of the interactive ideal, refuses to withhold personality long enough for the work to exert its character. This method weds itself to the repeating limitations of the single self, which projects onto literature a dispiriting sameness, an absence of any real variety. Whether the self chooses to play the adversary or the prince with his ready kiss, the self chooses the terms of interaction, to make of its account of reading yet another diary of relationship. By refusing, even for the moment, to subordinate itself, the self triumphs. The cost and prize are the same: it isn't changed. This method arises, possibly, to protest the ruse of disinterest, in the conviction there must be a truer way to read, a way less tainted by fraud. As indeed there may be.

But what is sacrificed with the ruse of disinterest is the opportunity to experience, briefly, no division between self and work, to become, briefly, nothing that is not that work (as Stevens might have had it). That the moment abandons us does not diminish its clarity and force; that it begins with pretense or disguise does not undermine the reality of its gift: perception, even flawed perception, of a universe and, sometimes, the pleasure of accurate homage.

THE BEST
AMERICAN
POETRY 1993:
INTRODUCTION

The world is complete without us. Intolerable fact. To which the poet responds by rebelling, wanting to prove otherwise. Out of wounded vanity or stubborn pride or desolate need, the poet lives in chronic dispute with fact, and an astonishment occurs: another fact is created, like a new element, in partial contradiction of the intolerable. Indelible voice, though it has no impact on the non-human universe, profoundly alters human experience of that universe, as well as of the world of relations, the solitude of the apparently marginal soul.

We know this happens: literature is its record or testament. A chilling word, literature. It gives no sense of the voice's adamant vitality, preferring to treat the poem as a distilled thing, inert and distant. Whereas the voice that rises from the page is wierdly restless: seductive, demanding, embittered, witty. Speaking not from the past but in the present. And it still happens: voices emerge from which, in Jeffers' phrase, fire cannot be leeched, whether because external change creates them or because they manifest the old drive with new emphasis or because there is in them some quality or force not yet identified.

It would be interesting to know something about that quality, because the poem, no matter how charged its content, will not survive on content but through voice. By voice I mean the style of thought, for which a style of speech—the clever grafts and borrowings, the habitual gestures scattered like clues in the lines—never convincingly substitutes. We fall back on that term, voice, for all its insufficiencies; it suggests, at least, the sound of an authentic being. Although such sound may draw on the poet's actual manner of speech, it is not, on the page, transcription. The voice is at liberty to excerpt, to exaggerate, to bypass what it chooses, to issue from conditions the real world will never exactly reproduce; unlike speech, it bears no immediate social pressure, since the other to whom it strives to make itself clear may not yet exist. The poem means to create that person, first in the poet, then in the reader. Meanwhile, its fidelity is not to the world: it need not provide a replica of the outward, or of social relations. This is why time confers more readily on the apolitical novel political significance: nineteenth century romantic novels, for example, were not necessarily conceived as political statements; they become such statements in light of the contemporary readiness to politicize gender relations. Also, an intuition that poems must be autobiography (since they are not description) unnerves the reader for whom the actual and the true are synonyms.

Poems *are* autobiography, but divested of the trappings of chronology and comment, the metronomic alternation of anecdote and response. Moreover, a body of work may change and develop less in reaction to the lived life than in reaction to the poet's prior discoveries, or the discoveries of others. If a poem remains so selectively amplified, so casual with fact, as to seem elusive, we must remember its agenda: not simply to record the actual but to continuously create the sensation of immersion in the actual. And if, in its striving to be free of the imprisoning self, the poet's gaze trains itself outward, it rests nevertheless on what compels or arrests it. Such choices constitute a portrait. Where the gaze is held, voice, or response, begins. Always in what follows the poet is alert, resistant, resisting dogma and fashion, resisting the greater danger of personal conviction, which must be held in suspicion, given its resemblance to dogma.

Still, for poems to touch us, we have to be magnetically drawn, we have to want to read these things. What makes this possible, what are the characteristics of those voices that, even as they become epigraphs or inscriptions in stone, mock the stone and the page with their vitality? Not, I think, that they sound beautiful or speak truth. Of these claims, the second seems at once grander and more accessible because of the ease with which truth identifies itself with sincerity as opposed to insight. Art's truth is as different from sincerity's honest disclosure as it is different from the truth we get in the doctor's office, that sequence of knowns which the doctor, newly trained to respect the patient's dignity, makes wholly available, affording, in the process, glimpses into a world of probabilities and strategies, the world of action transposed to conditions in which action can do only so much. The poem may embody perception so luminous it seems truth, but what keeps it alive is not fixed discovery but the means to discovery; what keeps it alive is intelligence.

No one disputes the desirability of intelligence. Many afternoons on the playground are ruined by assertions of its lack, many mornings in the charged classroom. The question is, how does it manifest itself, how does investment in truth constrain it?

The second issue first. Art is not a service. Or, rather, it does not reliably serve all people in a standardized way. Its service is to the spirit, from which it removes the misery of inertia. It does this by refocusing an existing image of the world; in this sense, it is less mirror than microscope—where the flat white of the page was, a field of energy emerges. Nevertheless, the absence of social function or social usefulness sometimes combines in the poet with a desire to serve, to do good: this absence and this pressure direct the poet toward the didactic. The teacherly, the wise, the morally sound, the noble: such utterance further soothes the poet's fragile ego by seemingly aligning his or her voice with the great voices, whose perceptions have been internalized as truth. But to make vital art, the poet must foreswear this alliance, however desperately it is sought, since what it produces is reiteration. Which is to say, not perception but the sensation of perception's endurance. And what is inevitably missing from such echoes is the sense of speech issuing in the moment from a specific, identifiable voice; what is missing is the sense of immediacy, volatility, which gives such voices their paradoxical durability. Whatever the nature of these voices, wherever they occur on the continuum between the casual and delphic, insight, as they speak it, feels like shocking event: wholly absent and then inevitable. And it comes slyly, or with an air of being unwilled, the air of query or postulate or vision.

In the reader, at these moments, an idea is being attacked, and the attack exhilarates. The old idea, not so much formulated and cleaved to as tacitly assumed, in its unclarity neither recognized nor repudiated, is displaced by perception: so the actively felt rushes to displace the passively unexamined, unsettling everything that has been built on that ground, and the air turns giddy with possibility, as though a whole new territory in the mind had been suddenly opened. Nothing has been destroyed that continues to be prized—rather, space is added. What has been sacrificed or shed seems only opacity, a sluggish dullness. Even when the sensation that one's solitude is shared disappears, what remains suggests solitude's fecundity.

As for the poet: mere unease, mere doubting of received ideas, is never enough: the poem must, on whatever scale, dislodge assumption, not by simply opposing it, but by dismantling the systematic proof in which its inevitability is grounded. In other words: not "C is wrong" but "who says A has to lead to B?" High seriousness, in its common disguise as tedious sobriety, is one of intelligence's readiest targets.

The poem which mistakes noble utterance for perception, conviction for impassioned intelligence, has located a wisdom it means to confer on its readers. Although such a poem may be organized dramatically and will likely have its climactic moment, it lacks drama: one feels, too early, its intention. Nor does deep familiarity with its design suggest that the poem has tapped into myth: myth is not formula. Such poems substitute the adjective for the noun; they offer the world draped in mythic reference. But in their willfulness, they lack myth's fatedness, myth's helpless encounter with the elemental. Instead, everything has been invested in conclusion, in axiom, in heroic grandeur. Poetic intelligence lacks, I think, such focused investment in conclusion, being naturally wary of its own assumptions. It derives its energy from a willingness to discard conclusion in the face of evidence, its willingness, in fact, to discard anything.

This flexibility and this intensity of purpose give the sort of eerie steadiness of mind Emily Dickinson has; even poets who stray wildly, intentionally, display such steadiness, since its essence is attentiveness to the path of thought. Nor is this egotism: thought, liberated of preconception, has nothing to do with self. What self is so free as to be able to disdain all previously held belief? Great concentration is required: perception does not hold still, patiently waiting to be encircled and made famous. It is visible in part, in moments; like the particles at the end of the microscope, it moves.

The voice that never existed can issue only from the life that never existed, a life experienced (whether it be adventurous or hermetic) wholly and without sentimental simplification, the enduring general deriving continually from the accepted individual life.

I took on this project for three reasons. First, I was impressed by David Lehman's willingness to let me say a few words against it. Second, I thought it would be wholesome to actually read, for a year, everything published in American magazines; conceivably, information would check my tendency to generalization and wild hypothesis. Last, I recognized, in my habitual refusal of this sort of assignment, a kind of preening. I preferred the cleanliness of powerlessness, but the refusal of power differs from lack of power; it places one among that elect to whom a choice is given. This particular mode, this life on the sidelines, preferably the very front of the sidelines, with the best view of the errors of others, promotes feelings of deeply satisfying moral rectitude combined with an invigorating sense of injustice: the particular limitations and insufficiencies and blindnesses of one's own preferences are never exposed because those preferences are never enacted. I liked not participating in the tyranny of taste making; I liked using words like "tyranny" and "taste making" to describe enacted preference, while guarding for myself words like "purity". What disrupts this is whatever offer finally makes clear the conditions on which refusal is based. I continue to feel aversion to overt authority, but a moment arrived in which I could no longer persuade myself that avoidance and lack were the same: they differ as willed and unwilled differ, as Marie Antoinette differs from the real milkmaid; continuous refusal to exert public influence on behalf of what I valued seemed exposed as vanity and self protection.

Meanwhile, unease lingers, in part a response to terminology. I dislike the idea that a single mind, or even a collective bound together by common theory, should determine what is called best. Moreover, I do not believe that excellence always finds its way into magazines. Nor do I think that poets are served by the existence of another mechanism of ranking, however sweet recognition may seem. Hierarchy dissolves passionate fellowship into bitter watchfulness—those who aren't vulnerable to this are usually those who are regularly honored. What is essential is that we sustain our readiness to learn from each other, a readiness which, by definition, requires from each of us the best work possible. We must, I think, fear whatever erodes the generosity on which exacting criticism depends.

Some of these reservations have been countered by the pleasure of discovery; some of this criticism checked by new awe for editors of magazines: every year they do what I did for one year. The miracle is not that they miss something, but that they find so much.

I tried to read with perfect detachment and could not. Inevitably, we read best the work that seems absolutely fresh or the work of those poets whose oeuvres we know thoroughly—such knowledge provides a resonance which cannot help but inform the reading of any single poem. On the other hand, such knowledge does not proceed from indifference: it presumes interest. I faltered in other ways; I read most clearly at the beginning, before I began drowning. As for the tonic effects of this labor: the mind that inclines to paradigm needs more than a year's comprehensive reading to correct its bias.

This collection is limited to what was published in one year, in magazines. Which creates regrettable omissions: this book should not be regarded as an anthology of the memorable work of our period, but as a culling, a journal of twelve months.

Finally, I prefer teaching as a means to encounter the not fully realized, the sporadically wonderful. That context transforms the unrealized to the incipient. The magazines I read regularly offer examples of the extremely interesting, the very nearly remarkable. But I prefer to meet such poems as mutable forms, for which no destiny seems impossible.

Still, among the multiple interesting poems, the poems dull to me or inaccessible to me, the poems that were echoes of other poems, the poems of startling promise, there were voices that, in my reading, stood out, like the voice at the dinner table whose next sentence you strain to hear, and some of these may be the enduring ones, the voices time can't force life from.

The Dreamer
and the
Watcher

I have to say at once that I am uneasy with commentary. My in-
sights on what I perceive to be the themes of this poem are al-
ready expressed: the poem embodies them. I can't add anything; what
I can do is make the implicit explicit, which exactly reverses the
poet's ambition. Perhaps the best alternative is to begin in circum-
stance.

In April of 1980, my house was destroyed by fire. A burned
house: a reprimand to the collector. Gradually certain benefits be-
came apparent. I felt grateful; the vivid sense of escape conferred on
daily life an aura of blessedness. I felt lucky to wake up, lucky to make
the beds, lucky to grind the coffee. There was also, after a period of
devastating grief, a strange exhilaration. Having nothing, I was no
longer hostage to possessions. For six weeks, my husband and son and
I lived with friends; in May we moved into Plainfield village, which
seemed, after the isolation of the country road, miraculously varied,
alive.

At that time, I hadn't written anything for about six months.
The natural silence after a book. Then the natural silence imposed by
crisis. I was oddly at peace with it. What word did I use? Necessary,

appropriate—whatever I said, the fact is that for once I relinquished the anxiety which, in my mind, ensured the return of vision. That first summer after the fire was a period of rare happiness—not ecstasy but another state, one more balanced, serene, attentive.

Toward the end of June, I began writing again, working on a poem called "Mock Orange." Then that poem was finished; in rapid succession, over a period of about two weeks, I wrote twelve more. Such experiences are, in many lives, a commonplace. But for me this was unprecedented and unexpectedly frightening. I kept feeling the poems weren't mine but collages of remembered lines. When I thought otherwise, I thought such fluency meant I was going to die, not sometime, but very soon. At such moments, for the first time in my life, I wished not to write; for the first time, I wanted survival above all else. That wish had no influence on behavior. Other factors—twenty years of discipline and obsession—were more powerful. When, of itself, the seizure ended, I was left with a sense of direction, a sense of how I wanted to sound. I wanted to locate poems in a *now* that would never recur, in a present that seemed to me utterly different from my previous uses of that tense. I had tried, always, to get at the unchanging. But, beginning at this time, my definitions of *essential* were themselves altering. I wanted, as well, poems not so much developed as undulant, more fire than marble. The work I'd just done suggested these possibilities. Meaning, it suggested a method, a tone. The chief attribute of that tone, as I heard it, was urgency, even recklessness. . . .

In practical terms, in the period before the fire I had set myself certain assignments. In the gloomy, unproductive winter of 1980, I was sorting, analyzing, trying to identify in my poems those habitual gestures—signature rhythms, tricks of syntax, and so on—that had to be discarded, trying, at the same time, to see what constructions I had tended to avoid. I had made a style of avoiding contractions and questions; it seemed to me I should learn to use them. Both forms felt completely alien, which was encouraging. That is, I allowed myself to believe something profound had been addressed. My work has always been strongly marked by a disregard for the circumstantial, except insofar as it could be transformed into paradigm. The poems in *Descending Figure* aim at a kind of terminal authority: they will not be distracted by the transitory, the partial; they reserve their love for what doesn't exist. I expect that, to some degree, this disposition not to acquiesce will always inform my work: an aspect of character. An aspect, also, of the passion for form. But if writing is to be a discovery, it must explore the unknown, and the unknown, to me, was informality—contractions and questions specify the human, not the oracular, voice.

"Night Song" was written in the early part of 1981, about six months after the period I've described. It's not clear to me to what extent the poem reflects either these concerns or these events. I find traces of both in the lines. And yet, the poem could not have been predicted. All this is something like looking at an old photograph of a friend: you can see readily how that child came to be this adult. But it doesn't work the other way; you can't find in the blurred, soft face of an infant the inevitable adult structure.

The process of writing doesn't, in my experience, vary much. What varies is the time required. For me, all poems begin in some fragment of motivating language—the task of writing a poem is the search for context. Other imaginations begin, I believe, in the actual, in the world, in some concrete thing which examination endows with significance. That process is generative: its proliferating associations produce a broad, lush, inclusive and, at times, playful poetry; its failures seem simply diffuse, without focus. My own work begins at the opposite end, at the end, literally, at illumination, which has then to be traced back to some source in the world. This method, when it succeeds, makes a thing that seems irrefutable. Its failure is felt as portentousness.

"Night Song" began with its first stanza, heard whole. And a working title: "Siren Song." A seduction. Are all seductions riddled with the imperative? As I remember, I had been thinking, on and off, of Psyche and Eros, thinking specifically of the illustration which had introduced these figures to me in childhood: the mortal woman bending over the ravishing god. This image remained with me, an independent fact, so divested of narrative that for years I didn't remember that Psyche had to be pressured into this betrayal. In my mind, Psyche leaning over Eros stood for the human compulsion to see, to know, for the rejection of whatever comfort results from deception. The figures suggested, as well, the dilemma of sexuality: the single body split apart again, an old subject; the exhausting obligation to recognize the other as other, as not part of the self.

For some months, I had no idea what to do with this beginning. The lines did seem a beginning: they were a summons, after all. In some sense, the "you" at this point was myself. "The calm of darkness is the horror of heaven"—the lesson was the lesson I keep trying to learn. But the poem had, I thought, to be dramatic.

When work resumed (how, why, I don't know), it went quickly. The dramatic situation remains sketchy—perhaps there is not enough background, in both senses of the word. But the truth is I didn't care about how these people got to this beach, or where the beach was. I could imagine no answers to such questions that were not conventional. What compelled me were the figures juxtaposed by this reunion: Eros and Psyche; the dreamer and the watcher.

What's essential is the idea of reunion; there has been provided, in reality, an exact replica of dream. Which event presumably erases the need for compensation or escape. And yet two primary responses suggest themselves: one can repudiate the translation or, in a kind of exorcism, one may permit the actual to supplant the dreamed. But immersion in time is a shock, involving real forfeits—of perfection, of the fantasy of eternity. That shock could be predicted. The surprise is that there are benefits to this perspective. To someone who feels, however briefly, without longing or regret, life on the shore, the life of dream, of waiting, seems suddenly tragic in its implications.

"Mild expectancy": what can be wrong with that? The lover hardly seems to be suffering. In his fatigue, he relaxes easily into the natural cycle, whereas the speaker's conscious determination places her outside these rhythms. This determination to stay awake is fueled by terror; it is, throughout the poem, a continuous, an active, choice. Expectancy, the sign of a heart set on the future—suddenly this seems a grave misuse of time. To dream, to yearn, or, in the realm of consciousness, to plan, to calculate—all a waste, a delusion. To live this way is to slight the earth. Not that the future isn't *real*. The delusion lies in projecting oneself into it indefinitely. One cannot live both there and here.

What the future holds is clear enough: the beach, the night world are dense with presentiments. Everywhere is stillness, the stillness of sleep which cannot help but resemble the stillness of death. What life there is regresses, the gulls, by example, transformed into clusters of cells. This is a warning, the message being: time is short. I hope a reader senses, in the poem's slow unreeling, interrupted with recurring commands, the degree to which this speaker is subject to the lure of the regressive. Her urgency reflects her own desire to capitulate and, in this sense, she sings to herself to keep awake, like someone on a vigil, a firewatch. There is, to put it plainly, an aspect of this which is pure pep talk.

The worst this poem can imagine is "what happens to the dreamers." The worst is to sleep through a life. By definition, it doesn't matter what the lover dreams; if he dreams, he isn't watching. Nor has the speaker's "weakness" been cured forever. Forever is, in itself, the dreamer's word. As for the peace passion gives: it could be called courage. Among the residual gifts of love is a composure, an openness to all experience, so profound it amounts to an acceptance of death. Or, more accurately, the future is no longer necessary. One is not rash, neither is one paralyzed by conservatism or hope. Simply, the sense of having lived, of having known one's fate, is very strong. And that sensation tells us what it is to live without the restrictions of fear. Such moments, in a way, have nothing to teach; they can be neither contrived nor prolonged by will. What they establish is a standard. Not forever, but for once it was possible to refuse consolation, to refuse the blindfold.

"Night Song" issues from, is made possible by, a sudden confidence. Whether finally or briefly, the soul can expose itself to "the revolutions," the massive cycles and upheavals of time. This is the greatest freedom we can know; its source, in the poem, is love, but the experience itself, the sense of being no longer "compelled," is an experience of autonomy. The lover's alert presence is necessary to confirm these sensations, since such experiences must be tested, witnessed.

What the speaker wants is *presence*, not union, dissolution, but the condition which preceded it. The choice is not between dreaming and lovemaking (another escape of self) but between dreaming and watching. Simultaneous consciousness, in other words—the exultant recognition of one soul by another. The ideal of balance has replaced the fantasy of incorporation. Contact of this sort seems to exist outside of time, beyond the laws of earth: all motion, whether toward fusion or separation, ends it. Motion is the first law. And as surely as the speaker's state dramatizes one of the soul's primary aims—to exist distinctly, to know where it ends and the blur of the world begins—so will the conflicting aim be asserted as the wish to dissolve, to be allied with, absorbed into another. The drive toward oblivion seems to me (as to many others) not a symptom of sickness but a true goal, and this wish of the self to do away with the very boundaries it has struggled to discover and maintain seems to me an endless subject, however we may try to subvert its grandeur.

I don't think of "Night Song" as a love poem. Love is a stimulus, and the advantage of writing out of situations of this kind seems to me an advantage of subject and attitude: one can write as lovers speak, of what is crucial in simple language.

The underlying subject seems to me to be individuality, without which no love can exist—groups do not love other groups. Love connects one irreplaceable being to another: the payment is terror of death, since if each person is unique, each death is singular, an eternal isolation. That we have common drives is consoling, but to dwell on them is to evade the issue of ultimate solitude. The relationships, in this poem, of the various forms of oblivion, of dream to orgasm to death, are less important than the perception of oblivion, in any form, as noncollective. If the pronouns in the last line are changed to "we" and "our," the line is instantly cloying, conventional; the sentiment thus expressed is paraphrased many times in the archives of Hallmark. Even if the second person is retained and only the possessive deleted, the thought turns vague—that in the second instance the line is also destroyed as a rhythmic unit is another problem. "You'll get oblivion"; "We'll get our oblivion": despite extreme discrepancies of tone, both sentences express the idea that oblivion is an alternative to self. Total eradication or complete union. "Night Song" suggests that the oblivion we ultimately achieve is an outpost of solitude from which the other is exiled—your oblivion is not mine, as your dream is not. This last line makes a mockery of placation; it damns the wish it grants. Against the relentless pronoun, the verbs are drumbeats, infantile, primitive. If what we want is oblivion, we are all lucky.

A last point. We are given to assume that morality depends on a regard for consequences. To some extent, this is surely true. But the regard is felt as fear—in this light, morality appears a product of intimidation. If "Night Song" connects the idea of freedom to rejection of the future, what is diminished, emotionally, is greed. Not avidity, but compulsive acquisition, need projected into time, the self straining to predict and provide for all foreseeable deficiency. I think the word *free* has no meaning if it does not suggest freedom from greed. To live in the present must mean being unerringly decisive, but choice, there, is easier, not harder. I do not claim to live on this plane, but I can imagine it.

It was clear to me long ago that any hope I had of writing real poetry depended on my living through common experiences. The privileged, the too-protected, the mandarin in my nature would have to be checked. At the same time, I was wary of drama, of disaster too deliberately courted: I have always been too at ease with extremes. What had to be cultivated, beyond a necessary neutrality, was the willingness to be identified with others. Not with the single other, the elect, but with a human community. My wish was to be special. But the representative life I wanted to record had somehow to be lived.

Major experiences vary in form—what reader and writer learn to do is recognize analogies. I watched my house burn—in the category of major losses, this made only the most modest start. Nor was it unexpected: I had spent twenty years waiting to undergo the losses I knew to be inevitable. I was obsessed with loss; not surprisingly, I was also acquisitive, possessive. The two tendencies fed each other; every impulse to extend my holdings increased the fundamental anxiety. Actual loss, loss of mere property, was a release, an abrupt transition from anticipation to expertise. In passing, I learned something about fire, about its appetite. I watched the destruction of all that had been, all that would not be again, and all that remained took on a radiance.

These are, in the deepest sense, ordinary experiences. On the subject of change, of loss, we all attain to authority. In my case, the timing was efficient. I was in my late thirties; perhaps I'd learned all I could about preparation, about gathering. The next lesson is abandon, letting go.

Perhaps, too, in all this there were other messages to be heard. And perhaps "Night Song" sounds much more of a piece with my other work than this suggests. It wouldn't surprise me. It seems these are the messages I'm equipped to receive.

ON
STANLEY
KUNITZ

About a year ago, in a classroom, I was asked to comment on my training as a writer. So I talked about my remarkable teachers, first Leonie Adams, then Stanley Kunitz. In fact, I was being drawn out to confirm a theory, a parable meant to connect the person presented, the fierce poet in the display case, with the obliging, malleable girl I must once have been, the diligent student who, after cautious apprenticeship, boldly cast off authority in order to write the true poems, the poems of experience, not written to please. This is the formula: a young girl is rescued by good fortune or energetic labor from the coffin of gender, meaning supervision by men. That myth arose to explain a perceived reality. But no one myth can explain all reality. What I found interesting in that classroom was the efficiency with which the teacher, also a woman, rejected nuance in favor of clean categories and individual testimony in favor of a cherished conception. In any case, those years didn't feel like that. What they were, what they meant, what I would have been without them, is hard to say, as the relation of teacher and student is hard to summarize. When it goes well, something passes between these figures, a species of love, one of the very few whose limitations do not impose suffering.

I met Stanley Kunitz when I was nineteen, having studied for two years with Leonie Adams. Both taught at Columbia, at the School of General Studies. They were in some ways alike, or what I took from them was similar. Teaching is not a series of opinions to be annexed: both Adams and Kunitz taught habits of thought, severe, strenuous, passionate—the giddiness of great discipline and great ambition. I had stopped taking class with Adams over a difference in taste, not directly regarding my own work. One evening, she'd read what seemed to her a shockingly bad poem, then being much praised. That poem was, for me, an epiphany; it told me how I wanted to sound. And, obviously, Adams was not the person to help me sound like that.

I don't know if, at nineteen, I seemed malleable. Like all people with a powerful sense of vocation, I was concerned with what I could use; by some absolute rule I recognized those minds I needed. I was less concerned, being self-absorbed, with the degree to which, by exposing myself to other wills, I might myself be changed. That is, I felt it necessary that I change; I wanted to be more than I was. At what point is the self, the voice, so wholly realized as to make its every project sacred? Obsession with authority as a principle of annihilation preserves the individual at the expense of growth. Even twenty-five years ago, it seemed clear to me that if my talent was so fragile, so precarious, as to require insulation from the world, it would never produce what I dreamed of anyway. So I made a sort of contract: I was prepared to be changed, but only by instruments of my own choosing. In that choice, I was meticulous.

Kunitz was my teacher for five years. But teacher seems the wrong noun, or maybe teach is the wrong verb. It seems simultaneously limited and coercive, as though its end product were to be a treaty of perpetual accord. For five years I overheard a splendid mind engaged with words, with what was the most crucial involvement in my life. I saw a kind of rigor in practice, and thought the sacrifice of contentment (which I didn't have anyway) was well worth such serious joy.

As the myth contends, I wrote to please him. In this, he was one in a series of projections, beginning with my mother. But the advantage in trying to please Kunitz was immense: what he wanted was to be surprised. This meant that lines like the lines he admired in January would not interest him in March. His voice became that part of my own mind that has been, since childhood, the tireless drill sergeant saying *move, move,* but in his voice concrete criticism substituted for mortification: where my own mind said *you are a fool to have hoped,* which produced anguish and justified laziness, Kunitz's voice would comment on the weak line, the dull word, the specific opacity. Where I damned and abandoned, he exhorted and compelled in the way only an outside voice can, because it can be excused praise. I felt, much of the time, doomed and exhilarated, or, in practical terms, always very tired, like a salmon swimming against the current. I had, in Kunitz, not only a persuasive argument for stamina but a companion spirit, someone my poems could talk to. Because what was clear from the first was that nothing in them was lost on him. I owe a great debt to Leonie Adams, but in the most profound sense Kunitz was the first human being by whom I felt entirely heard and this fact was a source of endless happiness. It couldn't have been, the sensation couldn't have lasted, if it translated into blanket approval. I wanted approval, but more than that I wanted to be heard, which is, I think, a more convincing proof of existence. One scene in particular haunts me. And if it is, in fact, an image of rescue, what I would stress are the means of rescue:

Several years have passed. The classes at General Studies have ended; Kunitz has not yet begun to teach at the School of the Arts. The School of the Arts doesn't exist. But I am to send him poems, keep him informed as to the progress of my manuscript, which has for some time been moving from bored hand to bored hand. It is, for me, a very bad year. All my life, there have been periods of painful silence: this is something different. I am writing with unusual fluency, writing one poem after another, but each poem in turn fills me with terror. They are that bad—not badly written, but empty, forced, accumulating, as a group, into a devastating verdict. This verdict is bad enough as I think it; I cannot face hearing it spoken. So seeing Kunitz at some reading causes wild anxiety. I am chastised: why have I sent him no poems? I must promise to send him poems.

My next problem is that promise: the problem is I have to keep it. And part of me, the stoic who was once so ready to let the fragile gift wither, thinks maybe this is just as well, that sooner or later the worst has to be encountered. The other part of me counsels flight. But I send the work. And then, amazingly, am invited to Twelfth Street to discuss it. A most interesting turn. Because this is a man of honor: having read the poems, he still wants to talk to me. For the next week, I feel very strange, feel as I felt years later when a poem was praised for what seemed to me its weakness. I feel a superficial calm and deeper agitation. It appears that either Kunitz will tell me, kindly, gently, that I am not a poet, or that Kunitz has read the poems wrong, has made a dreadful error, and I am not sure which turn is the more painful.

The house, which I get to see under these black circumstances, is wonderful, filled with all kinds of fascinating objects, so that exclamation can legitimately postpone the inevitable conversation. We drink martinis. We talk about this and that. And I begin to think that perhaps I was the one who was wrong, that perhaps the poems were somehow eloquent and interesting, that perhaps they marked some advance I couldn't as yet take in. This was the only explanation for such extended amiability; Kunitz was not a person to refuse the difficult task, neither would he sadistically prolong it. I began to feel a liquid well-being; I felt, actually, better than I had in about a year.

The poems were spread across his desk. I was standing in the doorway, from which distance they seemed quite impressive, unquestionably numerous, definitely printed with actual words. What Kunitz said was, "Of course, they're awful." And then, "But you know that." I referred this information immediately to god. I told him if he existed I wouldn't cry. That was about all that could be asked, since it was clear that I was, finally, really in the nightmare.

The turn was this: Kunitz remarked, quite casually, that this didn't matter, that I was a poet. What he meant, I think, was something more precise, conservative and liberating, a concept wholly new to me. Not that the poems were of any worth, but that they did not constitute, despite their number, a prophecy.

We spent several minutes going through the work. Maybe we would save a few lines. We saved nothing; in relief and joy, I used all the daring words—trash, junk, fraud—which seemed no longer an admission but a victory, heady in the way writing was heady. It was immeasurably important to do this in Kunitz's presence. He had done two things: paid me the compliment of speaking the truth, and afforded me the opportunity to follow suit. To learn through experience. Or, more accurately, to affirm a lost perception—what I had felt writing, and in psychoanalysis. That whatever the truth is, to speak it is a great adventure.

INVITATION
AND
EXCLUSION

It never occurred to me that I wasn't going to write poetry until I read Wallace Stevens. When I was very young, reading Shakespeare and Blake and Keats, or when, in adolescence, I began reading Yeats and Eliot and Pound, my experience of reading invariably strengthened an existing sense of vocation. Because this experience, the fact that reading great poets increased my confidence, never varied, I had no reason to examine it. Then something completely different happened; then a door was shut very sharply. Reading Stevens, I felt I would never write, and because I didn't want this to be true, I had to look more closely at those early experiences, and at the new, to find the source of the verdict.

In the actual act of reading Shakespeare, I had never felt dwarfed. Emerson makes this point: "Universal history," he says, "the poets, the romancers, do not in their stateliest pictures—in the sacerdotal, the imperial palaces, in the triumphs of will or of genius, anywhere lose our ear, anywhere make us feel that we intrude, that this is for our betters; but rather it is true that in their grandest strokes we feel most at home. All that Shakespeare says of the king, yonder slip of a boy that reads in the corner feels to be true of himself." It could also be said that, in this process, the reader who himself writes feels no technical division from the master, that their union is complete, that simultaneously they create the work in hand. The thrill of reading contains the thrill of making; as a child, I felt myself the author of those songs I read, and Shakespeare a prior author.

So the encounter with Stevens was shattering. And, just before, I'd been reading Eliot. I had felt my presence essential to those poems. They're spoken in low tones, in whispers, to a companion or confessor; their strategies make of groping an aesthetic. They advance, they hesitate, they retreat: they enact *doubt* in language. The *cri du coeur* craves a listener, a single listener who becomes, by virtue of his absorption, Eliot's collaborator.

The reader, in a poem like "The Love Song of J. Alfred Prufrock," is sought. His role, in its highest form, fulfills the function of the savior, because salvation lies in resemblance: that is the maxim Prufrock lives by so mistakenly, if indeed it can be said that Prufrock lives; but the intuition is sound. Among other things, Eliot reveals, through Prufrock, the horror of uncreative isolation. That's the worst of shame, its capacity to isolate. Prufrock isn't stupid; he's smart enough to be afraid of everything. But he's lost the passion that would have overcome his indecision. He seeks relief of solitude in invisibility; his life is an aggressive assertion of his unimportance, a history of *not* doing, *not* speaking, *not* violating existing modes; all this not doing is synchronized to meditation, in the form of anxious query and undermining evaluation. Prufrock accepts existing modes, having inherited a pressure to perform certain actions, but the reasoning that underlay the pressure is lost. In his caution and genteel automatism, Prufrock attains indistinction; he remains unspecific, bodiless, unrecognizable. A portrait of an unidentifiable man is a portrait of many, of a culture. When I talk about being heard, reaching toward, about connection, through tradition, to a lived present, I'm talking about what Prufrock can't do; the figure adrift may not be Eliot, but he locates Eliot's concerns. This is a poem infused with yearning, as is nearly all Eliot's work. Even his famous passion for tradition manifests, in another way, a longing for completion, for linking, for correspondence. He locates himself *in relation to.*

What I'm talking about is tone, also. Which is, to the reader, the fundamental issue. That is, we don't follow poems as arguments, step by step. We grasp them entire, and what we first grasp is tone. Which is why Eliot is far less difficult to read than, say, Frost. Tone, in Eliot, is instantly heard. Whereas it is in this realm, the instruction to the reader, that Frost plays his subtlest tricks: he eludes, he lures us into mistakes; finally, it requires enormous concentration and nerve to determine the informing emotion, or even the bias.

In any case, back in adolescence, I was used to reading poems that appeared to need to be heard, in that they postulated a listener. To seek moral instruction is to desire reply. And Stevens, at least in those poems I came to know first, didn't.

Stevens' meditative poems are not addressed outward; they are allowed to be overheard. That is the nature of meditation: the speaker and the listener are one. But to overhear is to experience exclusion; reading Stevens, I felt myself superfluous, part of some marginal throng. This capacity to efface is not a function of high language; neither is there an assumption of broad audience which emphasizes the inadequacy of the solitary reader. The difficulty to the reader is a function of the poem's mode, its privacy: to be allowed to follow is not to be asked along. Think, in this context, how full Eliot is of invitations, of pleas, of questions. And of constraints. There's a spaciousness in Stevens; a poem like "The Idea of Order at Key West" mimes the unimpeded progression of thought under no exhibited stress. Ideas *occur* to Stevens, fed by random associations, but the magnificence of the poem belies the process it represents by excluding all mistaken turnings.

The issue is not the presence, or degree of presence, of the personal. Eliot's masks and Stevens' sublime monologist suggest parallel restraints: neither poet seeks to make of himself a recognizable figure. It may be, however, that to celebrate imagination, the perceptive capability of the human mind with its deep alchemical impulse to transform, to make art, is to suppress the need for an other.

Prufrock is full of confusion; he doesn't understand what he sees. The world, for him, is a world of signs without meaning; but he expects—this is the point—to understand. Of course, Eliot isn't Prufrock, but you cannot be so alert to a species of agony without having felt it. Which is to say that, for the poem's purposes, Eliot isn't Prufrock, but the degree to which Prufrock resembles Eliot's subsequent speakers is extraordinary. Witness, for example, the points of correspondence between this poem and "Ash Wednesday." What's striking is that resemblance isn't confined to a single area, but asserts itself in diction, in the constellations of images, in dramatic movement. Perhaps this is not so terrifically surprising, in that Eliot's persistent subject is the cul-de-sac, one component of which is the trivializing of greatness, in "Prufrock": "In the room the women come and go / Talking of Michelangelo." Or, in "Ash Wednesday" locomotion to like accompaniment: "Who walked between the violet and the violet / Who walked between / The various ranks of varied green / Going in white and blue, in Mary's colour / Talking of trivial things / In ignorance and knowledge of eternal dolour." Or the use of the recurring, anxious question: "Shall I part my hair behind? Do I dare to eat a peach?"; or, in "Ash Wednesday": "Shall these bones live?" Or the sea as a repository of some lost life: "I have heard the mermaids singing, each to each. / I do not think that they will sing to me. / I have seen them riding seaward on the waves / Combing the white hair of the waves blown back / When the wind blows the water white and black." And, in "Ash Wednesday": "The white sails still fly seaward, seaward flying / Unbroken wings / And the lost heart stiffens and rejoices / In the lost lilac and the lost sea voices / And the weak spirit quickens to rebel / For the bent goldenrod and the lost sea smell." Moreover, the speakers' characters are not unlike; both poems are full of assertions of scaled-down expectation. Prufrock says "But though I have wept and fasted, wept and prayed / Though I have seen my head (grown slightly bald) brought in upon a platter / I am not a prophet . . ." In part he is not a prophet because the age of prophecy is past, and he is a figure poignantly alert to the expectations of the time. But the reach continues; man is left with vestigial impulses. In "Ash Wednesday": "Because these wings are no longer wings to fly / But merely vans to beat the air / The air which is now thoroughly small and dry / Smaller and dryer than the will." Both poems are un-equal to progress; Prufrock's turning back becomes the wavering of "Ash Wednesday." And the desire for release through unconscious-ness persists, with Prufrock's longing for anonymity changing to a wish for forgetfulness. Both poems rely on incantation and repetition, with the repetition frequently modified to introduce polar elements: "Prufrock"'s hundred "visions and revisions"; "Ash Wednesday"'s "Teach us to care and not to care." Repetition is a delaying tactic in both poems; in both poems the speakers define themselves by what they are not: "Because I do not hope to turn again / Because I do not hope / Because I do not hope to turn / Desiring this man's gift and that man's scope / I no longer strive to strive towards such things." And Prufrock is not Prince Hamlet. Finally, the infinite randomness of the finite, of time, "time for you and time for me" darkens to the bleak consciousness of "Ash Wednesday": "Because I know that time is always time / And place is always and only place / And what is ac-tual is actual only for one time / And only for one place." The major structural difference between the two poems is that prayer replaces resignation. But, again, the measure of anxiety is the uncompleted cry, the lapsed utterance, which dramatizes the breach, the void: "Suffer me not to be separated"—what's left out is what faith has to supply, the confident preposition, and the noun following. The unfin-ished cry is a confession of loss, division, exhaustion, supplanted by the last line "And let my cry come unto Thee." This is like the obedi-ence generated by extensive torture, or the wish for blind deliverance that succeeds too much feeling.

The material world, clearly, is not Eliot's natural home; it can-not provide him what he seeks: the answer, the way, the key, that which is unchanging. Every object is a potential Rosetta stone, and all tremors and shifts, the earth's mobility, mock his effort to focus. The temporal world provides no gratification for such quests: to seek an answer is to yearn for the immobile. But the fact of this, of not being at home in the world, makes isolation terrifying and fosters a violent need for the testimony of like souls.

Or like soul—soul in the singular. The plural is soullessness, society, the terrible engulfing human voices of Prufrock's last stanza. The annihilating, tidal power of the collective voice, like the cold, dismissive voice of the woman, before whose judgment Prufrock falters, corresponds to a desire for connection. The power to redeem and the power to destroy, whether real or projected, always coexist.

It is, in fact, individuating voice that Prufrock doesn't have, no longer hopes to have; he had to borrow a voice to speak. Prufrock's best hope is a complete abandonment of presumption; he can only hope to be annexed by some larger spirit. To concede identity, to see oneself in the role of attendant lord, comic, servile—this is tragic event, diluted because prolonged. It presents, also, a version of those feelings exalted in religion.

In "The Idea of Order at Key West," the woman singing by the sea sings in isolation, for her own pleasure. The communicative function of the voice is not what draws Stevens: the solitary singer is self-absorbed; her voice is not reaching toward conversation. Music is not speech. And the human voice, here, is the artist's instrument, an instance of "the maker's rage," the rage to order, to give or discern form: this is another species of religion entirely. And the poem is a poem of independence—the independent figure of the singer, the song itself, which becomes an environment, a made thing independent of its origins, subsuming, mastering those origins. Origins, which are so important to Eliot, are here secondary. The song is sung, and it is impossible not to stand in awe of a process so majestic, so exhilarating, so conspicuously private.

It would seem that the poet who makes this astonishing triumph for the individual voice would somehow encourage the individual reader. In my experience, this is not so. And not because of what Stevens says, but because of how he says it, and to whom.

Unlike Eliot, Stevens is not alarmed by diversity. Nor is he concerned to understand the nature of the sea. The sea is an occasion, a stimulus; Stevens looks to the world for those arresting configurations which stimulate the creative process. Shift doesn't frighten him—the more shifts, the more configurations. If you treat objects as icons, presuming some inherent significance, you presume, likewise, the universal applicability of that single significance, and this assumption of common ground links the poet to the reader. If, however, objects are occasions, and the notion of inherent significance secondary, beside the point, if it exists at all, then all weight, all import, is conferred by the perceiving eye. And what is stressed is that eye, the individual intelligence. And as the poet's imagination becomes increasingly unique, its creations increasingly liberated from their sources, so the reader is reminded of the poet's self-sufficiency.

When, in "The Idea of Order," Stevens turns finally to another intelligence, when a second view is apparently solicited, he turns to someone other than oneself, someone of whom the reader has never heard. The fact that among the many Ramon Fernandezes—and there must be many, since the name combines a common Christian name with a common surname (common, that is, in another culture)—the fact that there finally turns up a Ramon Fernandez prominent enough to have entered a poem, means very little. That man is not Stevens' man; when Stevens requires a companion, he makes one up, with his usual resourcefulness.

If exclusion, in Stevens, is tacit, in the later work of Sylvia Plath it is most violently active. Plath's poems renounce human aid, human analogy—this contempt resembles not at all the proprietary obsessiveness of much contemporary poetry which stakes out territorial claims based on personal history: my father, my pain, my persistent memory. Plath invests almost nothing in circumstance; rather, she consciously distinguishes herself in her response, and so converts the ordinary to the heroic. The Ariel poems are the obedient child's revenge, a fierce parody of acquiescence. That is, they comply with an existing stereotype, but they comply too vigorously with anticipated judgment; they confirm what they're expected to deny, the negative female archetype: dramatic, shrill, hysterical, bitchy. So they sabotage the war, since the adversary has learned to rely on defensiveness for his validation. The drama was supposed to go this way: the charge made, the charge refuted, and in the act of refuting those behaviors generated which confirm the charge. Plath becomes what she's accused of being, but she becomes deliberately; will displaces surrender.

The informing passion of "Lady Lazarus" is revenge, retaliation: when the dead come back with their grievances intact, they come back to haunt. This is the last resort of the helpless, and requires enormous sacrifice: the victim distills herself into an unkillable voice. This poem, like others of the period, is saturated with a willed unwholesomeness; what Plath has to do is repudiate the old imprisoning rituals which derive from the imposed primary association of Woman with Life. For her threat to work, though, she has to produce a kind of receptive insecurity in the enemy by undermining basic assumptions, for example, the assumption that smiling women are smiling through and through, are tame, or that the dead stay dead.

There are two obvious entries into poems: respondent and analogue. The latter is, in "Lady Lazarus," regularly forbidden. The speaker here has already outdone Lazarus' unprecedented return by having managed it more than once: what was event to him is routine, in both senses of the word, to her. Though one wouldn't necessarily know this; appearance doesn't prove it. Like Clark Kent, Plath moves through the world camouflaged by her apparent lack of distinction; she claims something else; she claims secret distinction. She performs in disguise, as a young, smiling, conventional woman. But the invitation to analogy, which must include not only the mask but the heroic, ascendant fury—that invitation is a taunt. We haven't passed the first test; we haven't died. Everywhere here is that resistant, mercuric quality: you think you know me, the poem says. You don't know me; you can't even imagine me. Which is to say, we're hearing someone out of our range.

One of the most remarkable things about this amazing poem is its complete absence of hesitation and, in consequence, its complete authority. This is masterful theater, but the point is that what we're watching is not a performance in a play, in which a sympathetic bond is struck between actor and audience. What we're watching is a magic act, and its success depends on the unbridgeable distance between artist and audience; for the trick to work, the beholder has to be ignorant.

This means, in a way, that there is no audience, at least there is no audience capable of appreciating the complexity of the trick, no audience sufficiently aware of its audacity, or of the boldness or stylishness of its execution. It seems to me that here is one of the great differences between Anne Sexton and Plath, if we put aside the issue of talent: Sexton presumes connoisseurs and plays to them. She also relishes belonging; her obsession with suicide was obviously genuine, but it reads as oddly social; there's something in the work of the girl who got into the best club.

Whereas Plath severs all ties. If "Lady Lazarus" records the eruption of a subterranean life, it is, nevertheless, the antithesis of the haphazard. Plath insists on the idea of control; everything must seem to have been chosen. Even the agonizing return "to the same place, the same face, the same/ brute amused shout" attests to the speaker's nerve; this is the hard part of the trick, the "comeback." But routine, utterly expected. All of it, the wildness, the will, the daring, is intended to obscure the simple fact that there never was a choice at all. Nevertheless, the whole force of this poem is bent on exclusion; the superiority of the poet consists of her scorn for consolation, her refusal to concede resemblance.

Like Plath, Emily Dickinson is a poet of private anguish. Unlike Plath, she sometimes writes in code; some of the poems are completely hermetic, impenetrable. But *not* exclusive, in the sense I mean. Selective, rather; these poems are like messages in bottles; they are designed to be discovered. And, though profoundly self-protective, meant to be understood. It is hard to think of a body of work that so manages, without renouncing personal authority, to so invest in the single reader. Dickinson seems, sometimes, the elderly lady scrutinizing the young face: she's looking to detect blood relationship. The scrutiny, the caution, the extreme selectivity resemble Marianne Moore's to put it backwards. But Dickinson's intensity and concerns speak of the crucial, not the interesting.

Plath rejects human analogy and so exiles the reader. Dickinson simultaneously invites and elevates, though the tone of the search varies: it can be imperial, discriminating ("The soul selects her own society . . .") or coyly collusive ("I'm nobody! Who are you?"). But the poem I want to look at beside "Lady Lazarus" is a poem in which the invitation works more subtly, because the specific need for an other is not its central objective.

Plath requires attention in order to deny her need for help. "Lady Lazarus" is full of spectacular effects, sound effects; the unremitting intensity calls attention to the furious triumph. A negative triumph, since the victim has the power to destroy rather than the power to be. Dickinson's intensity is of another sort; "great pain" generates muteness, silence transferred to the mouth by the stunned heart. In this regard notice the use of the definite article, which functions two ways. We don't have "my nerves" or even a more decorous form of possession, like "one's nerves." "The nerves," here, have a separate life; the mind, the soul, no longer supervise, drawing everything together under the rule of an I. In the traumatized, dying animal, some parts live longer. Meanwhile, in the poem, all sense of time is gone. Here, in microcosm, is Yeats' center that doesn't hold: the nerves sit, the feet go round, but there is no organizing core, no government. This is, I think, the article's main effect. Secondarily, the reader is permitted immediate access; analogy can be assumed. Because Dickinson doesn't specify *her* nervous system. And we trust the poem regardless, since we recognize high-quality information.

The poem, moreover, goes on to move in widening circles. Great pain, in Plath, resurrects the violent ego which renounces comparison, being obsessed with boundaries. Dickinson manages to be both intensely personal and devoid of egotism; in a sense, the poem is *about* being devoid of ego. But I want to stress a more technical point: the poem resolves in a search for precedent, or analogy. Freezing persons who survive that state probably do not make up any large human category. But the point is the way imagination's used; the ego-less speaker exerts imagination to connect herself with the species. This extraordinary final image clarifies by analogy; it also dignifies projection as a mode.

It occurred to me to wonder what all this comes to. That is, I want to say something practical, pragmatic. So I will discuss for a moment a rather strange process, which these remarks attempt to illuminate.

The poems from which I feel excluded are not poems from which I can learn. Neither are they poems I can ignore. I suppose I ought to define learning, the sort I mean. It has to do with license, absorption, momentum, and is unlike the repetitions of mimicry, which are mechanical and stationary, which lead nowhere, that is, which lead solely to the poem they echo. I think of those poems the reader co-authors as places occupied, and, therefore, as points of departure. The calm of possession produces appetite for change: those poems in which we participate free us from the need to rewrite them. They also encourage, though this encouragement is not always felt as the immediate rush to compose. If I describe my own sensation, I would say these poems confirmed an existing hope; they fostered the sense that I had it in me to write. In fact, that was the exact experience: I had, in the act of reading, had it in me.

My definition of learning depends on seeing a difference between that appetite for change and the process of anxious duplication. Those poems we passionately admire but never fully occupy have to be converted into tenanted space; they must be occupied to be points of departure. And the only means of conversion is dogged imitation, which is always deficient and never works and can go on indefinitely, because we so need to fend off the implicit judgment. And we work always facing the monument, so as to re-create it perfectly. But the monument remains the monument. Or the obstacle. And the poems we write in this state are the dead products of fear and inhibition; they have no author at all.

DEATH
AND
ABSENCE

What strikes me is how far away all this work seems, not only the poems that are literally remote, that go back twenty years. Once a poem is resolved, I lose the sense of having written it. I can remember circumstances, but not sensations, not what it felt like to be writing. This amnesia is most immediate and most complete when poems are written quickly, but in all cases it occurs. Between poems, I am not a poet, only someone with a yearning to achieve—what? That concentration again.

The oldest poem here is "The Racer's Widow," lines of which were written when I was about fifteen. The best lines, in fact, though at that time the subject was different. Occasion might be a better word, for reasons which will become clear. In its first embodiment, the poem described the last agonies of a deer. I didn't know very much about deer, but then I didn't know very much about racing, either. The problem with the poem was that its declared subject was a fraud: my interest did not begin with a deer but with a metaphor. From the first, I wanted to talk about death; also from the first I had an instinctive identification with the abandoned, the widowed, with all figures left behind. I'll come back to this; the point now is that, in this early poem, the widow was a doe. So the poem, as a whole, was mystical to the point of absurdity. Yet something in the language seemed true and deep: the legs "like snow" and so on. My problem, for years, was that I didn't know what these lines might describe. This is, for me, often the case: miraculously, some word or phrase will detach itself from the language; the task of writing is a search for context. I don't remember how, four or five years later, I hit on the persona here. But I had begun to read modern poems, that much is clear.

"Cottonmouth Country" dates from this same period—from about 1963. Because it was written quickly, I have no memory relating to its composition. I did go to Hatteras; there was an actual snake. But those events seemed utterly without importance; at the time, they didn't even turn into anecdote. They emerged, months afterward, not as potential but as completed metamorphosis. This is the process of dreams: small details and forgotten incidents surface there, releasing some latent significance.

Poems of this kind are, for me, fairly rare. The other poems must, through effort, be made to sound so spontaneously whole. Much such effort is represented here, long intervals of frustration. The longer poems did not, always, take longer to write, but the two here raise a particular issue. Because in each case the subject matter is felt to be both personal and charged, these poems have sometimes been praised for their bravery, which is not my word, as though their writing put an end to years of evasion. I have a great appetite for praise, and would like to be considered brave, but the term as used in this case results from misperception. The poems were not written sooner because, in both instances, resonance was missing. The original experiences had to be not simply assimilated but converted. Bravery was never at issue: I tried regularly to make poems out of these situations since I recognized their possibilities. These poems, these many attempts, were frank but without mystery. The problem was tone: toward my sister, toward the syndrome of anorexia that for years shaped my life, I kept taking appropriate attitudes, when what was wanted had to be, in some way unique. In any case, obsession is not courage.

I have always been, in one way or another, obsessed with sisters, the dead and the living both. The dead sister died before I was born. Her death was not my experience, but her absence was. Her death let me be born. I saw myself as her substitute, which produced in me a profound obligation toward my mother, and a frantic desire to remedy her every distress. I took it all personally: every shadow that crossed her face proved my insufficiency; the birth of my younger sister proved this yet more concretely. At the same time, I took on the guilty responsibility of the survivor. Everything was wrong—it seemed wrong to forget the dead child, impossible to attend her. I knew these things, as articulate insight, twenty-five years ago. They did not become the material of poetry until, at thirty, I had a child myself. The wild, protective, terrified love I felt for my son—that maternal love which, in being obsessed with protection, is obsessed with harm—transformed itself, over three years, into an analogous act of mourning. "Descending Figure" is saturated with a mother's grief and fearfulness and a haunted child's compulsive compensation. It means, also, to *study* maternal love, which continued to seem to me appalling, though I felt it. Originally, the second section, which describes a hypothetical painting, began: "That embrace, I ask you/does it guard or restrict?" In the end, those lines were cut: they summarized what the poem had to suggest. Of the three, this section was written last, and with the greatest difficulty. I had pretty much given up hope of drawing together the two existing poems about my sister, and was working on, trying to infuse some energy into, an ironic little poem about sources of illumination: the painting was made up to accommodate what I wanted to say. It was a fruitless exercise, until I thought of the poem in connection with "The Wanderer" and "For My Sister," Once this idea presented itself, the inert, shallow lyric with its chest and winter stars became an excitement, borrowing urgency from the poems it would link.

As the editor of this volume knows, it has taken me a long time to write these paragraphs. I don't trust my prose, except in letters. My stake in poetry is immeasurable, but, oddly, this fact, like some ideal of service, arrests egotism. I have no such vision in prose. And whereas a letter gives me someone to address, a public occasion of this sort makes focus impossible. But "vision" and "focus" miss the point, though they make plain what is missing: I thought once that poems were like words inscribed in rock or caught in amber. I thought in these terms so long, so fervently, with such investment in images of preservation and fixity, that the inaccuracies of the metaphor as description of my own experience did not occur to me until very recently. What is left out of these images is the idea of contact, and contact, of the most intimate sort, is what poetry can accomplish. Poems do not endure as objects but as presences. When you read anything worth remembering, you liberate a human voice; you release into the world again a companion spirit.

I read poems to hear that voice. And I write to speak to those I have heard.

ON
IMPOVERISHMENT

I am here to talk to you about the future. For the speaker, this occasion makes a kind of Rorschach test, twenty minutes being insufficient time in which to describe the long interesting lives we all hope for.

The future is not assured; that is its drama. It can show itself in two shapes: as ongoing reality—a present extended indefinitely—or as a new world. In the second case, a boundary asserts itself, making a culmination or transition. To stand at that boundary is to be divested of the past, which for the first time, in its distinctness, needs to be called the past. At first this perception feels exhilarating and dangerous and infinitely fresh: the past is fixed, achieved, and no longer binding—it cannot be farmed for insight.

In my own life I have found that a certain psychic condition succeeds this exhilaration. Its sign is impoverishment, a sense of inertia that owes something to the past's increasing remoteness, a loss of connection to the accomplishments which occurred there, but more, I think, to the impossibility of projecting alternatives, of imagining an occupied future. Some of you may have felt this already, after long enterprise, after closure or triumph, after fatigue, after pride in achievement ebbs. Suddenly the present seems an agony; what has been lost is the self, that construct of memory and vision which so depends on a stable conception of the past, a stable trajectory into the future.

The terror of this condition is that it has lost the power to yearn, while remembering a time when this was not so. It yearns only for respite, meaning release from hopelessness; it can imagine no more specific objective. Moreover, such confinement represents itself not as a tunnel, a darkness being passed through, but as a well; it is a place time cannot reach. Because response to the world is no longer actively felt, change—which is inherently active—seems impossible to imagine. This profound sense of having nothing, of being incapable of thought or response, this desolate emptiness runs contrary to every hope we have for ourselves; its atmosphere of finality reproduces the sensation of arrival that characterizes triumph, and mocks that sensation. At the same time, interior paralysis magnifies external vitality: all around, other people seem enviably caught up in, animated by feeling.

In the late sixties, I was living in New York, writing the poems that would complete my first book. I want to read the last poem added to that manuscript, not because it is good but because it begins a narrative. It is a poem I would never otherwise read aloud:

LA FORCE

Made me what I am.
Gray, glued to her dream
Kitchen, among bones, among these
Dripping willows squatted to imbed
A bulb: I tend her plot. Her pride
And joy she said. I have no pride.
The lawn thins; overfed,
Her late roses gag on fertilizer past the tool
House. Now the cards are cut.
She cannot eat, she cannot take the stairs—

My life is sealed. The woman with the hound
Comes up but she will not be harmed.
I have the care of her.

As you can probably hear, the poem is all endings, its sentences
fragmented, often lacking subjects, like dolls with their heads cut off.
The poem has ferocity without depth; it seems finished before it be-
gins, before any dramatic situation declares itself. Its subject is fate,
the immutable; its ferocity the anger of protest. To the degree that it
is dominated by that subject, it *is* finished before it begins, resolved
before it begins, the evolution of any dramatic situation pointless. The
poem was written in 1967; it reads to me now as the degeneration of
a set of discoveries into a set of mannerisms. At the time too, I believe
I sensed that, sensed some vision—of language, of human relations—
had played itself out.

Four years later I moved to Vermont, having accepted my first
teaching job. I took the job four days before the semester began; col-
leagues found me a place to live, a bedroom in a rooming house, a
wonderful room with orange paisley wallpaper and a huge four poster
bed, a cross between old New England farmhouse and bordello. Let
me read the first poem I wrote in that room:

ALL HALLOWS

Even now this landscape is assembling.
The hills darken. The oxen
sleep in their blue yoke,
the fields having been
picked clean, the sheaves
bound evenly and piled at the roadside
among cinquefoil, as the toothed moon rises:

This is the barrenness
of harvest or pestilence.
And the wife leaning out the window

with her hand extended, as in payment,
and the seeds
distinct, gold, calling
Come here
Come here, little one

And the soul creeps out of the tree.

You can hear, I hope, immense change. Though the second poem is preoccupied with fate, emphasis has shifted from the specific unalterable to the eternally recurring. For the shards and fragments of "La Force," the end-dominated phrases, this poem substitutes dreamy suspended sentences; for verdict and judgment, it substitutes deferred interpretation; for the restrictions and intensifications of brutally narrowed perspective, it substitutes a hovering all-seeing eye. It is, I believe, a much richer poem, different not only in style but in quality.

A reader encountering two disparate works is encouraged to speculate about what the poet might, in the intervening years, have been reading, what events might have occurred in the life to so transform an aesthetic and—implicitly—a character. In fact, I was reading nothing. I opened and closed books, I leafed through them, but their failure to move me accumulated into desperate anxiety. And it seemed at the time that, in my life, nothing was happening, or nothing with any power to change me. I moved from New York to Provincetown, from Provincetown to Vermont. I had a few turbulent relationships. But nothing I read, nothing I saw or heard provoked response. And in the absence of response to the world, the act of writing, which had been, which is, the center of my life, the act or dream that suffuses the life with meaning, had virtually stopped. For two years I wrote a little, three or four poems in all, and these seemed no more than treading water. For two years, I wrote nothing, not a word. It seemed increasingly impossible to remember a time when I had been fully alive, impossible to imagine a future in which I would live that way again.

It was a period of great panic and helplessness. Because my life seemed over, I made decisions based on small things: I moved to Vermont because I liked the people there, and because the gift I had been protecting by refusing to do anything as potentially distracting as teaching—that gift seemed to have left me. As it turned out, teaching was absorbing but not distracting; it made a place for me to put to use abilities I thought had atrophied.

I tell you these things to prepare you, to encourage you, but preparation does not preclude suffering. The question isn't whether or not you will suffer. You *will* suffer. At issue is the meaning of suffering, or the yield.

To teach myself hope, I began, thirty years ago, to chart periods of silence in the same way that I dated poems. And I have repeatedly seen long silence end in speech. Moreover, the speech, the writing that begins after such a siege, differs always from what went before, and in ways I couldn't through act of will accomplish. And this happens even when outward circumstances don't change at all. Some work is done through suffering, through impoverishment, through the involuntary relinquishing of a self.

Despair in our culture tends to produce wild activity: change the job, change the partner, replace the faltering ambition instantly. We fear passivity and prize action, meaning the action we initiate. But the self cannot be willed back. And flight from despair forfeits whatever benefit may arise in the encounter with despair.

Unfortunately, it doesn't follow that, since despair can sponsor deep change, capitulation should be immediate and absolute. The condition demands resistance at the outset; to treat impoverishment as a prerequisite to wealth, to turn it into a kind of fraternity hazing, is to deny the experience. It must be feared and resisted; it must exhaust all available resources, since its essence is defeat.

The alternative? A life made entirely of will and ultimately dominated by fear. Such a life expresses itself in too prompt, too superficial adjustments of what can, in the external environment, be manipulated, or in a cautious clinging to those habits and forms which, because they are not crucial, cannot, in being lost, do much damage. The deft skirting of despair is a life lived on the surface, intimidated by depth, a life that refuses to be used by time, which it tries instead to dominate or evade. It is all abrupt movement or anxious cleaving; it does not understand that random action is also a kind of stasis. In its horror of passivity, it forgets that passivity over time is, by definition, active. There exists, in other words, a form of action felt as helplessness, a form of will that exhibits, on the surface, none of the familiar dynamic properties of will. Fortitude is will. Can it be taken too far? Yes—but the same argument can be made against all action: when response becomes policy it has ceased to engage directly with circumstance. And I suppose patience, in its various forms, is particularly susceptible to this deterioration.

It is very strange to stand here, wishing you desolation, like the bad fairy at the cradle. You have, all of you, a vocation for learning. And you have been well taught here. Realize, then, that impoverishment is also a teacher, unique in its capacity to renew, and that its yield, when it ends, is a passionate openness which in turn re-invests the world with meaning. What I remember of such moments is gratitude: the fact of being born immerses us in the world without conveying the daily immensity of that gift. To live in the world in the absence of such knowledge may not be tragic: I don't know; I have no prolonged experience of such a life. But I think some intensity of awareness must be lost, since it depends on contrast. And that intensity is impoverishment's aftermath, and blessing: what succeeds temporary darkness, what succeeds the void or the desert, is not the primary gift of the world but the essential secondary gift of knowledge, a sense of the significance of the original gift, the scale of our privilege.

—*Baccalaureate address, Williams College, 1993.*

ABOUT THE AUTHOR

Louise Glück teaches at Williams College and lives in Vermont with her husband and son. She is the author of six books of poems and is the recipient of the National Book Critics Circle Award for Poetry, the Boston Globe Literary Press Award for Poetry, and the Poetry Society of America's Melville Kane Award and William Carlos Williams Award. In 1993, she received the Pulitzer Prize for her book *The Wild Iris*.